CORO

A Nove

by

David Arrowsmith

Copyright David Arrowsmith 2020

For my daughter Ivy

Copyright © 2020 David Christopher Frank Arrowsmith
The right of David Arrowsmith to be identified as the Author of the Work has been asserted by him in accordance with the Copyright, Designs and Patents Act 1988.
First published in 2023.
Apart from any under UK copyright law, this publication may only be reproduced, stored, or transmitted, in any form, or by any means, with prior permission in writing of the publishers or author, or in the case of reprographic production, in accordance with the terms of licenses issued by the Copyright Licensing Agency.
All characters in this publication are fictitious and any resemblance to real persons, living or dead, is purely coincidental.

CONTENTS:

PART ONE: CONVERGENCE

PART TWO: CHAOS

PART THREE: DIVERGENCE

MAP

CODA

BONUS CONTENT

PART ONE
CONVERGENCE

THE MAN

He eases up the garage door as quietly as he can, spraying tiny squirts of lubricant on the hinges as he gently tilts, painstakingly inching it up and open. His eyes take a second to adjust to the gloom of the single room lock-up within. It's another sunny day, like almost every day it seems, but in the small garage that he uses as a storage unit it's cold, dark and musty. He scans the piles, mentally taking inventory of his depleting stock. Pallets of tins are piled precariously on top of one another, the exposed cardboard and torn cellophane now outweighing the remaining tins themselves. He tours the garage, selecting a can here, a jar there. He pauses in front of a locked trunk, pushed into the corner and half-covered with a mouldy old tarp. Pulling out his keys he opens the small padlock and surveys the contents, almost untouched since all this began, since she left and the world turned to shit.

A four pack of toilet paper - quilted. Tinned tomatoes, dried pasta, UHT milk, hand sanitiser, plain flour. All the stuff that got scarce and then disappeared altogether. And then what passed for survival staples - matches, candles, water purification tablets, a small green pouch containing a mini first aid kit. He's resisted using any of it, part of his constant efforts at self-discipline. Or perhaps something else. Nothing taken out, and just one item added, since her departure – his fingertips grazing the nap of the small velvet pouch, now tucked snugly into the far corner of the lock box.

Something makes him freeze, crouched with his hand halfway to closing the trunk. A noise perhaps? He doesn't move, breath held, muscles trembling as he strains to make out what triggered his barely-checked automatic flight response. Hearing nothing further he carefully closes and locks the trunk, and slowly stands and turns to face the open door once more. Looking out of the darkness is like being inside a pinhole camera. The outside is so bright and crisp and clear it's almost hyper real. He can feel what he hopes is not a migraine coming. Time to go.

He scans the area and, seeing nothing amiss, closes the garage door - but not without banging the bottom edge on the concrete floor with a clank that echoes across the car park. Everything seems louder these days - without the constant background noises they took for granted before all this: the trains at Denmark Hill station, the regular procession of passing buses, the sirens of the ambulances racing to and from King's College Hospital, the drone of passenger planes transporting the masses to their holiday destinations of choice.

He sets off for the mansion block that towers above him at a brisk walk, the tins and jars clinking in the pockets of the oversize raincoat. An uncomfortable sweat spreads across his back. He can feel the moisture sticking his threadbare clothing to the skin under his arms, across his neck and in the hollow of his lower back.

This time he's sure. That's a noise. A stick snapping underfoot. Maybe twenty metres away, to his left and behind him. He doesn't stop, or turn to look. He just runs. He's tall and slim and his long legs stretch out to eat up the ground between here and the door to the block. But, as he rounds the corner, skirting the flower bed where the rose bushes stand prickly guard, he skids wide - the leather on the soles of his shoes worn thin and frictionless - and one foot slides off the pavement and into the gutter, his ankle rolling painfully. He's able to right his foot and regain his stride instantly, and without falling, but the burst of pain bodes ill.

***

13th December 2020

I'm not sure why I'm still writing this diary. I guess I've always been a completist: 'I've started so I'll finish' as that old television quiz master – what was his name again? - loved to say. I guess it gives me something to do. Sometimes it feels like therapy (bit late for that, right?), but I also want it to be some kind of record, to stand as a monument to what happened, for better or worse. Who knows maybe one day someone (you, Lucy?) will read this...

I shudder to think what the world is like for you, dear reader. I wonder if you were even alive 'before', if you even know what it was like for those of us who experienced it. Sometimes I imagine that you're reading this in a world where the slate has been wiped clean – and that those memories, for so long preserved in printed word and cached ones and zeroes, in hearts and minds and living recall, have gone, lost forever like everything else. Perhaps this diary is the last surviving testament. If it is, then know you will find precious little of worth within these pages. But today, if I do one thing, I would like to do my best to set down the story – for it is only a story, we are past the point of an objective truth, if ever such a thing existed – of the fall of man.

It came from China. Wuhan. Something to do with the "wet" markets there, where they just wash the animals' blood and guts into gutters and drains at the end of each day. Bats and pangolins coming into contact with each other and creating a new virus that can attack humans. Or that's the prevailing belief anyway, what the news said, back when there was news. I could never quite bring myself to discount the rumours about a Russian bio research lab that had an accident a few months prior though. It just seemed like there was a plausible New Cold War motivation for almost everything that started to go wrong across the Western democracies. At least to me anyway. Then again, I've always loved a conspiracy theory. It's not like I was one of the Luddites who had started attacking mobile phone masts when the serious whack jobs claimed it was all caused by the new 5G cell phone networks though. They needn't have bothered. 4G, 5G, wifi, it all went down in the end.

Whatever the source of the outbreak, it made the jump to humans and started causing illness and death in Wuhan. A particularly nasty kind of flu that attacked the lungs and respiratory system, it seemed deadliest for the old, the weak and the sick. From Wuhan it spread across China, aided by a lack of transparency that ran pretty close to being a cover up. As a result, no one here was really aware of it until too late.

Eventually it swept the globe and, nation by nation, the death toll rose and the lockdowns began.

To begin with it was just low-level stuff. Lots of deaths, yes, but a pandemic on the normal, albeit horrific, scale. Some panic buying and shortages, outbreaks of minor criminality, lockdowns in most countries turning the planet's major cities into ghost towns. Manchester, Liverpool, London – each and every major town and city in the UK eventually fell into the most serious 'tier 3' category, before they had to invent a tier 4, then a tier 5...

The global death toll was well into the millions. For those of us that had survived, life went to shit. And, just when I thought it couldn't get much worse, Lucy left.

But it was when the second spike came that the trouble really started...

The assumed immunity never materialised. Those that had had it before got reinfected. And somehow it was worse the second time around. Perhaps the lungs had already been damaged and weakened, in readiness for the virus's second onslaught. All attempts to flatten this second curve and control the timing of this second wave failed. It was like a viral tsunami, making landfall bang in the middle of flu season, with our hospitals already full of the sick and elderly. Doctors and nurses dropped like flies. Ventilators, PPE, everything ran out within days despite the previous months of production and stockpiling. The deaths skyrocketed and the morgues and cemeteries couldn't keep up. The proliferation of corpses caused all kinds of secondary illnesses and fatalities as the plague gained the ascendancy.

As more and more people succumbed, from all walks of life and professions, the infrastructure and amenities of major Western powers ground to a halt and collapsed. Britain was no exception. In London refuse stopped being collected, and piled in the streets with the bodies of the dead. Gas, electricity and water supplies across the country were turned off, or failed catastrophically, or became so intermittent that they could no longer be relied upon. Food supplies dwindled, as imports and exports ceased and domestic production faltered and stalled. There were shortages of everything. The skeleton emergency services could no longer maintain control as the riots, lootings and criminality spiralled out of control.

London became a post-apocalyptic war zone. Criminal gangs took over the cities, patrolling their territories while the rest stayed locked up inside.

***

THE MAN

One such gang has seemingly decided to camp out in front of his block of flats, a handful of them now sitting around a pile of wood that they have got burning with the help of petrol siphoned from parked cars. The global market had collapsed early on - oil values had turned negative and, with vehicles rusting and airport runways abandoned, never recovered. The once 'black gold' was now less than worthless, except as a pyro accelerant.

He can see them from the balcony of the top floor flat they once shared, where he now stands alone amongst the potted plants, taking in the impressive London skyline from this unique geographical vantage point high up on Dog Kennel Hill as the sun sets once again.

He's lived there for five years now, four years BC (before Corona). Most of that time with Lucy and then, latterly, alone. When they'd bought the flat, they'd had to jump through all kinds of hoops to pass the residents committee tests and win over the neighbours. Most of those friends, and foes, were now dead.

Lucy had left in the summer, before the second outbreak. Before the descent into total anarchy and lawlessness that had now become the new normal.

Now it's just him and Mr. Tibbles.

Closing the balcony door behind him, he pulls out the tins and jars and packets from his pockets - more than any one coat should have, some original, most repaired, several carefully sewn in for additional carrying capacity over the last nine months. Eventually, from a flap right underneath a damp armpit, he plucks the gaudy packet of dried cat food. As he rips the spout open and pours a measure into a plastic bowl the cat appears and, with a cursory lazy blink, sidles past and tucks in. Before he stows the pack in the cupboard he tosses a couple of pieces into his mouth, clears his throat, and swallows them down, encapsulated in a tiny glob of mucus.

Dinner is served.

***

THE MAN

Up on the flat roof, he limps heavily between the pots and pans arrayed over the surface, checking to see if any overnight rain has replenished them. The sun is barely peeking beyond the distant skyline of St Paul's cathedral, the London Eye, The City - and the wispy cloud cover has yet to burn off. He shivers, and pulls the overcoat tighter around his gaunt frame. It's hard adjusting to being so skinny when you were always more on the "cuddly" side, but he's been fastidious in rationing himself almost since day one - certainly since Lucy left anyway. That and the regular calisthenics exercise regimen he's adopted - cobbled together from vague memories of a mother with a Rosemary Conley workout DVD, and the basic stretches and exercises Lucy used to force him to do to stop his back giving out - means he's fit but whippet-thin. At least that means less weight on his painfully swollen ankle.

Should probably look at that properly now that it's daylight again.

As ever, there are no planes in the sky, no vapour trails anywhere to be seen. Not even any helicopters ferrying urgent medevac patients to the rooftop helipad of King's hospital. The sky has belonged to the birds, and the birds alone, for months.

Then the walkie talkie, habitually clipped to his frayed rope belt but perpetually forgotten, crackles into life. He always keeps it charged, semi-regularly changing the frequency and broadcasting a welcome message just in case he can make contact with anyone monitoring locally. Or in the faint hope that Lucy tries to reach him with the sister handset he gave her as she left. He's never been contacted, by Lucy, by anyone. Never had any response at all.

As soon as he hears her voice his head starts to spin. He sees the distant metal spire of the Crystal Palace transmitter shear across his eye-line as if toppling to earth. As his vision narrows down to two tiny pinpricks of light, the peripheral images blurring and turning black, he crumples to the ground in an undignified slump. He avoids further injuring his ankle but can't help but bang his tailbone. She's saying something about a baby. Before he can force his parched vocal cords into a response, she's telling the airwaves that he shouldn't try to find her, that she'll broadcast again when the child is safely delivered.

Is that a siren? From the handset, or the road down the hill? Or both? I must be projecting again. It's getting louder and louder, as if it's right here on the roof with me...

The migraine breaks out in its full, brutal and all-encompassing glory – just as the handset crackles and dies, and the sun finally bursts free of the horizon, and the low-lying clouds, and beams directly into his skull. All he can hear is static and the pulsing of the blood in his temples.

When he finally risks opening his eyes again the sun is high in the sky, but mercifully shielded from direct view by a picture perfect fluffy white cloud. He tentatively massages his temples with his fingertips, unfurls from the foetal position, rolls awkwardly onto his knees and eventually, gingerly, stands up, favouring his injured ankle.

Any water there might have been in the pots and pans is long gone. The walkie talkie handset is dead, its battery depleted. The world is silent, save for the spontaneous outbursts of cheerfully naive birdsong, as it has been for almost all of almost every day for nearly a year.

As the migraine fades it is replaced by the realisation he's not just thirsty but dangerously dehydrated, and his stomach is cramping and spasming.

***

THE MAN

He eases the door closed, pushes up the nub on the latch, turns the key in the lock and slides the well-oiled bolts at the top and bottom across. Peering through the bleary fisheye of the peephole for a full minute, he sees nothing in the corridor.

He carries the handset over to a car battery - salvaged from his car, before the gangs had finished stripping the entire car park - that now sits proudly on the Formica kitchen counter top like a fancy Italian coffee machine. With the walkie charging, he picks some leaves from a proliferation of plants growing on the balcony and sets them stewing in a pot atop a camping stove.

In the bedroom he pulls a battered leather-bound journal from under the pillow, and a canteen from the bedside table, and carries them back to the living room. He sits down in a collapsible fisherman's chair at the metal folding camping table and the book falls open, a plastic biro from a distant holiday rolling out, the bright yellow sun logo revealed anew with each rotation.

He speaks the words as he writes, taking a tiny sip of water from the canteen when his voice cracks and breaks:

2nd May 2021

She must be close. Range of the walkies is what, a mile? Two, max. Which means she must be having the baby (my baby???) at King's. I heard something, an ambulance maybe, from the roof. Could it be for her? Then again, why would anyone use a siren? Suicide to draw that much attention to yourself. Maybe I'm hearing things again. The migraine was a bad one. Maybe I imagined the siren. Maybe I imagined her?

Either way, I've seen enough activity to know there are some survivors over there - even the odd occasion when they've used the ambulance to get through the cordons of gangs. Supply runs? Picking up sick or injured, or recruiting?

She's heading there. She must be.

I'd stopped writing in here, it seemed pointless. But this, this is surely worth recording...

***

THE MAN

It starts as a faint scratching sound. Not enough to have woken him, that must have been the pain radiating from his ankle. But enough to keep him awake, and on edge, now. He slows his ragged breathing and focuses on the noise. Just as he's homed in on it, it stops. The herbal tea and poultice don't seem to have done much except leave a bitter tang in his mouth and a damp patch on the dirty pillow he's using to elevate his ankle.

He hasn't had a working watch or clock for weeks, not since the battery died in the bedside radio alarm clock that hadn't played the radio, or beeped an alarm, since it all happened. But judging by the fact that the sun was now casting large horizontal shadows from the Venetian blind across the room it must be late afternoon. Maybe sixish.

He rolls onto his side and sits up on the edge of the bed, keeping his injured foot an inch above the mattress until it's clear and he can rest it gently on the floor. The poultice slides off, unnoticed. He's once more distracted by the noise. Scratch, scratch. And is that a squeak?

***

THE MAN

He checks the rucksack contents one more time.

Fully charged walkie. Canteen (half full). Kendall mint cake. Wind up torch. Zippo (almost completely out of fuel). Imitation Swiss Army Knife with a faulty compass and broken primary blade (why didn't I fork out for the real deal?).

He's survived this long by being quiet, and careful and solitary. He's eked out the supplies he "reappropriated" from a closed down Spar - a smash and grab job with his neighbour Tim, a former lawyer whose idea it was and who drove the van through the shutters - and supplemented them with scavenged goods and homegrown herbs, fruit and veg. Tim died maybe six months ago. Or at least that was the last time he saw him. And the next day he'd seen one of the local gang members wearing his watch.

He'd never been in the army or the TA, not even the Boy Scouts (he'd quit after his Cubs troupe disbanded). And he had hated the awful away days and team bonding session they always insisted on at the office. Paintballing. Orienteering. Lucy always made him go, said he shouldn't look like the odd one out. But he *was* the odd one out. And that was all the more obvious every time he was made to participate in those exhausting charades. Still, the backwoods survival weekend had ended up saving his life several times over since he'd been fending for himself. Even though he'd hated every cold, wet and windy second of it, something must have stuck. Maybe it was the young female instructor who reminded him somehow of the Lucy he'd first started dating all those years ago.

He tucks a battered hip flask and his diary into the rucksack's elasticated side pouch, then pulls the flask back out. He unscrews the stopper and tentatively takes a tiny swig, sucking his teeth as the alcohol burns its way down his dried-out throat.

Another noise. It's so quiet these days that he can pick up anything happening in the block. Not that there's been a peep for days. As far as he can tell, with Tim gone, he's the last one left. So, this is strange. Is he really hearing it? Sounds - scraping, possibly footsteps, even what seems like voices. Then a heavy half-bang half-thud and the sound of splintering wood. It's on his floor. Maybe two doors down, definitely on his corridor. They've finally exhausted the local houses and returned to loot the top floor flats they gave up on once the lift stopped working.

Sounds like only two of them. Still, they'll be done with that flat in no time, he doubts Mrs. O'Donnell had much left when she just walked off towards Elephant and Castle in her nightdress talking about plantains. Sure enough, another crashing noise, this time the door of the flat next door.

He sweeps up the rucksack, scans the room for anything he's forgetting and inches through the half-open balcony door. He's barely had time to move more than a handful of his plant pots out of the way before he can hear them getting ready to break down his door. A running jump, weaving through the plants and stuttering to take off from his good foot, and he's a hundred feet above the rose bed and halfway between his balcony and Tim's when the two men burst into his flat. His chest slams into the Victorian brickwork of the next-door balcony as his hands scrabble to find purchase on the smooth, curved top. Banging his knees hard he hauls his mercifully skeletal frame up and over and collapses on the tiles, hidden from any intruder who might peer over from his balcony.

He hears a whoop. They must have found his car battery. As he lies still, trying to bring his breathing and heart rate down and ignore the multitude of new and old competing pains, he finds his eyeline gives him a view into Tim's living room and, via the large and only partially cracked mirror on the wall, right through into the bedroom.

At first it looks like a giant teddy bear, or a fur coat draped over the bed. Then it moves, and he gets the whiff of a disturbingly familiar stench that he realises must have been around for months and he'd just learnt to ignore. Death. Decay. The rats moving over the body like a rippling wave.

Had he seen Tim since that day he disappeared? When was it, late December maybe? He remembers it now. It was Christmas Eve. He'd gone out to try and find a gift for Lucy. She'd already left to shack up with her very own survivalist, Barry - from her work team-building trip to the Peak District. But back then he had still thought he could win her back. Wanted to win her back. What the fuck happened to Tim? He's definitely dead now. Maybe not six months gone though. Could he have been living next door to him without realising?

He stops the cogs whirring in his brain, silencing the distraction of his scattergun internal monologue to strain for sounds from the intruders. If they decide to try Tim's flat next, he's really not sure he can make the jump back to his own balcony. It sounds like they might be almost done turning his little home upside down. He hears the squeak of his balcony door opening wide. He uses the noise to mask the tell-tale sound of the zip on his rucksack opening, and grasps the cheap knock-off penknife in one hand, opening the stubby secondary blade with the other.

He hadn't realised his eyed were closed, until he opens them at the sound of laughter so incongruous he has to stop himself joining in. Then the sound of pots smashing wipes the awkward smile from his face. He'd poured what little remaining love and energy he'd had since Lucy left into those plants. Well, he can't move back into the flat now anyway. And he wasn't really going to take them with him. Still, it makes him sad. Reminds him that the world really has gone bad.

He hears the men's laugher retreat, and tenses again - ready for the pounding on the next door. Tim's door. It never comes. Minutes later he hears the laughter again, but faintly this time, from far below. And again, a whoop, now echoed by more voices.

He peeks over the edge of the balcony to see the men, maybe eight of them, passing around the battery - and a couple of tote bags he recognises as Mrs. O'Donnell's, adorned with the logos of local, and long since defunct, businesses. Each tin, each jar, many of them clearly his, greeted with a roar of approval and the odd smash as an empty beer bottle is tossed.

His plants lie on the tarmac of the access road right in front of the main door to the block, a straggly pile of stalks and brambles and leaves, dotted amongst hillocks of soil and shattered fragments of pots of all colours. He allows himself a solitary tear before he ducks back down and tries the handle of the door that leads from the balcony into Tim's flat.

***

24th December 2020

That was awkward. Just had to close the door on Tim from next door. Think he might be losing it a bit.

Earlier he'd seen me come back from my covert trip to the high street. I had managed to liberate a necklace from the storeroom of the little jewellers Lucy likes so much. The display items had all been looted months ago, but when people realised that diamonds were far less valuable than food or water - or matches - attentions turned elsewhere. It was a risky trip and I nearly got spotted a couple of times by different local gangs, but if I'm going to try and win Lucy back I need a big romantic gesture. Anyway, he saw me come back and when I told him what I'd been doing it was like a little light went on in his head. Like in a cartoon. Right there and then he decided he'd make a dash for the toyshop, so he'd have a gift and might finally work up the courage to hike over to see his daughter.

When he finally reappeared, hours later, his trousers were all torn and bloody and he was bleeding profusely from his leg. It looked like he had a large shard or two of glass stuck in there pretty good. Turns out he'd come a cropper climbing in through the toyshop window. A patch of pale skin on his wrist where his beloved Patek Philippe was normally ever-present suggested something else might have occurred out there, but he gave no further indication of any human confrontations. Seemed a bit suspicious to me. I questioned him about it, and he got more and more agitated. Said he just wanted to borrow some stuff from my first aid kit to clean up, and maybe some antibiotics. He said he knew I'd grabbed some when we 'visited' the pharmacy. I told him I didn't have any in the flat (which was true). He was getting really worked up now, and I didn't want to give away the last of my medical supplies, so it all came to a bit of a head. He tried to barge in, so I pushed him back by the face and went to close the door - but it slammed on his bad leg. He was furious but I managed to shut him out and ignore his banging and pleading until he finally slinked back to his flat.

Time to cross Tim off the list, I think. That leaves officially no one as a reliable ally in here (except Mr. Tibbles, of course). He was always more Lucy's friend than mine anyway. Tim, not Tibbles. At least until Ange dumped him and took Thea off to live with her parents in Maidenhead. Lucy didn't seem to want anything to do with him after that but, as the world went to shit, he and I ended up sharing a few risky 'adventures'. More so after Lucy left me. Not any more though. Better to be alone. He's not right. I might reinforce the door tonight before I turn in. The wood from the dining table should do the trick.

***

THE MAN

The living room is thick and close with the stench of Tim's corpse, even though the body is around the corner in the bedroom. Bluebottles buzz lazily in the uncomfortably ripe yet stale warmth of a room that hasn't had an open window in months. The dust motes, catching the light and swirling in the gentle breeze from the now-open balcony door like bioluminescent plankton, make him feel like he's exploring deep under the ocean. He's brought jarringly back to reality as he forgetfully takes a heavy step on his injured ankle.

He catches sight of himself in the mirror - he destroyed his own a long time ago, in a fit of rage, or pity, or clarity - and barely recognises his pale, drawn features beneath the long, lank straggly hair and wild beard. He looks more like a consumptive cowboy from the old West than a former solicitor and failed husband. An ancient mariner, the albatross long since slaughtered.

In the bedroom the rats have gone. For now, at least. There's enough of the body left to see that Tim only has a single leg. He finds the missing limb where it must have rolled under the bed. It's too infected even for the rats to have touched it. Under the half-used roll of crepe bandages on the bedside table he finds a small, blunt saw – his brain deliberately skipping over the incontrovertible bloodstains - and then, just what he needs, the kitchen scissors.

He lets the hair fall where it may, on his shoulders or the tiled floor, as he hacks it first from his head and then from his face. The banging, the screams and shouts, the whimpering, the raving - it had been easy to shut it out in the end. Surprisingly so. The thick old walls had helped.

***

LUCY

She paces the room, passing in and out of the alternating shadows and patches of light where the bin bags taped to the windows have torn and peeled away. She holds the handset in one hand, resting atop the bump that has stretched the threadbare material of her top so thin it's threatening to tear, the other cradles the baby in her belly from below. She bites her lip absentmindedly as she goes over her words again. Did she do the right thing in even contacting him? Well, he knows now. He deserves to know, even if she couldn't bring herself to tell him as much. Better leave it ambiguous. Especially as she *really* doesn't want him there. This is her baby and hers alone. She's managed this far. Thankfully she got Barry to show her how to use the back-up petrol generator to charge things like the walkie talkie - she'd never used it, or changed the frequency - before he left.

It had been better with him gone somehow. She just wasn't meant to be cooped up for that long with another human being. At least not with a man. Not with Barry. As autumn had turned to winter, and the second wave had obliterated everything in its path, they had enforced their own extreme survival lockdown. But then all the good things about him seemed to become negatives – and multiplied and magnified until she couldn't stand anything to do with him or his stupid fucking face.

She'd learnt what she needed to from him - how to scavenge food, siphon petrol, collect and purify water. He'd been the one who'd discovered the outpost at King's – a doctor or doctors, maybe nurse or paramedic, hard to tell, but they'd occasionally spied the ambulance rolling past silently on the streets, a dark form hunched behind the wheel, peering - and had found out the frequency. She'd finally kicked him out then. He'd wanted to go for a while, she could tell. But he was too much of a coward to say it. He'd had enough of looking after her, let alone a baby that he suspected wasn't his.

She'd waited as long as she could, weeks judging by the lines she'd gouged on the wall to mark the passing of days. For the longest time she'd debated the pros and cons, risk and reward, of contacting an outsider. But today she was pretty sure the contractions were starting. And suddenly, if only for a fleeting moment, she'd felt more scared, more alone, than she had thought possible. It had been enough. The voice, a man she was pretty sure, had said the ambulance would come, that she wasn't far and that she'd be ok. Damn right she'd be ok. But there was no sign of them. How long ago did she contact them? It felt like hours.

Fuck this. Time for the mountain to go to Mohammad.

***

THE DOCTOR

He tosses the portable ham radio set onto the passenger seat, closes his eyes, mouths a silent prayer to whatever higher power might be listening, and turns the key. All he gets in response is a faint, flat ticking sound.

Come on. Not now.

He's already late, got side-tracked helping moving one of the old guys to a different bed while he was trying to find the grab bag for the ambulance.

He hates running behind, especially when it's a live one. That's assuming it was a genuine call. The woman had sounded pretty calm for someone claiming to be in labour. And the last time he'd answered an emergency call out from an unknown female he'd only narrowly escaped a gang ambush. Since then, he'd reinforced as many of the myriad entrances to the hospital block and its underground car park as he could, grouped as many of his patients as possible into the private suites on the top floor, and abandoned all the empty levels in between.

He tries the key again. With a roar that seems terrifyingly loud in the echoing confines of the underground parking garage, the engine bursts into life. The shock of the noise startles him, his left hand slipping from the wheel and striking the siren switch.

He flips it back off immediately but not before an ear-piercing whistle is projected from the vehicle at three hundred and forty metres per second, racing through the car park and out into the world, amplified by a giant concrete speaker.

Fuck fuck fuck.

He holds his breath, grips the steering wheel and waits. Nothing happens. No one appears at the top of the exit ramp, where the broken barrier arm lies propped against the empty guard booth.

He waits longer, forcing himself to count to a hundred. Still nothing.

He puts the vehicle in gear and presses down on the accelerator pedal as softly as his exhausted muscles will allow. Creeping forward, he waits until he's clear of the building before he engages second gear, and then third.

The lack of side view mirrors, lost so long ago he can't even remember what happened to them, means as the ambulance glides away he fails to notice the man slipping into the underground garage behind him.

***

THE MAN

The wind is bitingly cold. The weather has seemed purer, more intense, since the very beginning. First it was clear skies, blue and sunny with not even a vapour trail. Then the winds came. Pollen, grit and sand - and rubbish, all whipped through the narrow streets and passageways. Once he'd nearly been decapitated by an off-cut of wood - and had retraced it's flight to find a discarded skip from a long abandoned renovation project that was an Aladdin's cave of supplies to keep his flat warm, safe and secure.

He'd discovered the rear exit fire door ages ago, but it only opened from the inside and he never risked keeping it propped open when he was on a supply run just in case one of the gang spotted it. Force of habit means he quietly pushes it to once more, scans the area one final time to check all is clear, and then moves, insect-like, through the untended tangle of grass that had once been the communal rear gardens. His frame is set against the biting wind, coat pulled close and rucksack strapped tight, but his are eyes sparkling and his hair blows freely in the breeze.

The last few weeks have been like a fevered dream. The migraine had eventually faded to the background but the exertions of the last twenty-four hours, coupled with his growing hunger - something he'd been unable to satisfy since the gang raided his flat - have left him feeling a strange combination of euphoric and on edge. As if gliding through a dream that's teetering on the edge of a nightmare. He'd only tried drugs a handful of times, and normally it was Lucy egging him on when they were at some painfully dull social event - but this had been a bit like that. Only worse. And better.

Now, out in the open and moving (albeit painfully) with a real purpose, he finally feels like he's starting to wake up. The wind, for so long the bane of his sorties out beyond the block of flats, is "blowing the cobwebs away" as Lucy would have said. It helps that he has no real choice. He'd always known he'd have to abandon the flat eventually, the gang had shown no sign of moving to new hunting grounds and it was only a matter of time before he was discovered. They'll know he can't be far, have been able to tell the flat was very recently occupied. The portable stove was probably still warm to the touch, and there were clues all over the place - from well-tended plants to fresh dirty dishes in the sink.

But now, finally, he has a destination. A purpose. King's. Just get to King's. And don't think about the fact that Lucy said she didn't want him to try and find her. Block that out. Like Tim's screams. Or the other dark and shameful things he'd done to survive this long.

He just has one more thing to do before he sets off on the half-mile journey to the hospital. Even with a limp, getting to King's from here should only take him a couple of hours or so. The biggest challenge is staying unseen - it necessitates a longer, more circuitous route and a certain level of concentration and caution. Getting anywhere in one piece is painfully slow.

He cuts across the grass verge and presses himself flat against the wall of the building. Kneeling down on the dried bark chippings of the flowerbed he cranes his neck to peer around the corner. It takes him a minute to refocus his eyes, blinking and concentrating until he can will them to obey. He almost wishes they hadn't. The lock up is once again bathed in sunshine. But where the battered and rusty door should be there's just a dark gaping maw. Scraps of cardboard and cellophane are scattered outside. As the wind picks up, they start to slide across the concrete until they get pinned against the wall of another line of garages at the far end of the car park. The incessant, mocking birdsong jars his nerves.

There are no signs of anyone else around. And none of the other garages have been broken into. He crouch-limps across the ground, keeping to the shadows cast by the trees - trees that haven't been pruned by the council tree surgeon in nearly two years now. Maybe he should have done that. Worked with plants or trees. It's not like being a lawyer had brought him any joy. He'd been busy when Corona first hit - the lawyers were in demand for mergers and acquisitions, employment issues, furloughing and redundancy claims, all kinds of economic and social fallout from the initial soft impact of COVID-19. Then, when it got worse, so much worse, there wasn't much use for any white-collar work at all. Who needs a lawyer when there aren't any laws anymore? The trees were still there though.

The lock up had been well and truly ransacked. Whoever it was either had help or some form of transport - no way one person could carry all that stuff. No chance now to have a morale boosting breakfast before the journey. Then he sees the tarpaulin, cast aside. The bottom falls out of his stomach, like when his dad used to drive too fast over the bumpy roads on their childhood trips to the countryside. The chest has been forcibly pried open. It's empty. He just stares. Not really at the box. Not really at anything. Just a hazy, glazed stare into the invisible middle distance. He fights the urge to be sick. The effort brings him back to his present reality. There's nothing here. He needs to leave.

***

6th December 2020

My supplies are running perilously low. I've been eking what little I had left for weeks now, ever since I declined that last supply run (raiding party more like) with the proto-gang that's sprung up around here. I can see them devolving before my eyes. One sortie with them was enough, there was something too gleeful about their embracing of the violence of our actions. It wasn't just a vital expedition to source food, water, medicine – it was a chance to give a show of force, to scare off any lone stragglers still in the neighbourhood and to mete wanton destruction on property. Yes, we found some tins and jars and bottles – the spoils of war divided up between us when we got back to the flats – but this wasn't just about survival, this was about something else. Something darker. They could tell, I think, could see my unease, my tacit withdrawal. I've managed to avoid them all since then. I'd rather try and do this on my own. But I'm not sure they'll let me...

***

LUCY

It's not easy walking when you're nine months pregnant, let alone carrying all your own supplies and trying to move quietly and carefully to remain unheard and unseen. The old beach bag is awkward, it keeps sliding off her shoulder and banging her bump, but it was the only thing she could find that was big enough for the various bits and bobs she wanted with her. Now she just has to make it to the hospital, and hope they're there and able to help her.

She'd always been organised. When she'd got pregnant the first time she'd already made a list and pre-packed her bag long before the final hospital visit, when they found out she wouldn't need it after all. Maybe that was the start of the end for them. It wasn't too long after that she met Barry. Anyway, she'd never used that first bag, but the list had stayed burned into her memory. It made her packing and clearing out of the maisonette this time that much quicker. Just as well, as the contractions - she was pretty sure that's what they were - are definitely getting more intense and closer together.

Another one builds and she has to stop and lean against a building. The bricks, warmed by the sun, feel wonderful beneath her palms as she flattens them against the wall. She bends almost double, her bump rising to meet her face. She remembers when she could touch her toes. Or at least see them. Yoga was a lifetime ago. A different world.

Oh fuck that's painful.

Her lip is bleeding as she bites down hard to stop herself screaming. She grinds the top of her skull into the wall in a vain effort to distract herself with a different, more manageable kind of pain. Opening her eyes she sees the crimson blood form a perfect circular spatter on the dusty pavement, and has a moment of total panic before she realises it's dripping from her mouth.

When the contraction finally passes, she's too exhausted to walk any further. Her back to the wall, she slides down into a sitting position. She has just enough energy and presence of mind to reach out and grab the wheelie bin beside her and drag it closer so she can rest against it and be partially hidden from view if anyone passes the entrance to the alleyway.

***

THE DOCTOR

He's sure this is the place. But the door is closed and there's no sign of life anywhere. The windows are all taped over with some kind of black paper or plastic, and he's been hunched over the steering wheel, staring at the torn corners for what seems like hours now and he's spotted not a single movement, no flitting figure or moving shadow or glint of reflected light.

It's silent except for the near-constant background burble of birdsong, something he'd long ago tuned out. In the beginning it had been a joy, the return of birds in a variety and quantity not seen since he was a child. Bluetits, robins, sparrows, blackbirds, pigeons, magpies, the bright green flashes and exotic calls of the wild parakeets. He'd enjoyed cataloguing them in his breaks from tending his patients. His dad would have loved to see that, God rest his soul.

The commotion as a pair of blackbirds fight off an opportunist magpie brings him back to the present. She's not here. If she ever was. She'd sounded so real. Or maybe he'd just wanted her to be.

He hadn't noticed their approach. Two young men, hoods pulled up over their heads despite the heat, masks over their faces that are definitely not surgical grade but look more like Halloween items from the Camberwell fancy dress shop.

Fuck. Not again. Fooled you twice, dickhead.

The ambulance starts first time and he slams it into reverse, watching through his grimy windscreen as the youths shrink away. Then there's a thud and a bump, and a sort of crunch or crack that goes right through him. The two lads, if they are indeed young men - it's not always easy to tell, the way some of the urban gangs dress - share a masked look in the distance. He moves the gear stick into first and tests the accelerator pedal. The pair split, loping off in opposite directions like jackals reassessing their choice of prey.

He's not convinced they've really gone, but he risks leaning right over and cracking open the passenger side door. Peering down past the footwell, his chin resting on the side edge of the seat, he can just about make out what can only be one half of a Scream mask.

Oh no. No no no.

He finds him under the front left wheel, hood wrapped tight around the axel, the remaining half of the mask still on, the sharp broken edge gouged into his face. He's still breathing. Little red bubbles appear and burst at the exposed corner of his mouth as his chest rises and falls. No sign of the others.

He opens the back doors of the vehicle, cringing as they squeak audibly in the silent street. Surgical scissors cut through the hoody easily, then the elastic straps on the mask - although it doesn't fall off at first, the flap of skin it has inserted itself into holding it in place until he tugs it away in a veil of thick, slow-moving blood. The body slides out easily enough and he gets it onto the stretcher as quickly as he can, glancing over his shoulder at each little positioning tug. He's so exposed, even more than last time. He'd sworn he'd never let that happen again. Knew he had to be smarter than that. Tougher than that. And here he was. Again. Only worse. For a smart guy he really did never learn.

***

LUCY

A screech of tyres, and a strange popping, snapping sound, bring her to her senses. How long has she been slumped on the ground, leaning against a bin? A wave of contraction seizes her and takes over her senses, every active part of her brain. There is only the contraction. She is the contraction, and the contraction is her. She does her best to focus and breathe - some of that hypnobirthing podcast must have stuck after all. Not that it really seems to help. How on Earth has mankind not found a better way than this to reproduce?

As the radiating pain finally dissipates a shadow briefly disorientates her. A battered ambulance freewheeling past the alleyway entrance, a deep red smear spattered from front wheel arch to window sill - as if it had got stuck in deep, wet clay and struggled to get free. Before she can decide if she's hallucinating or not the vehicle has gone and the realisation she's all alone, with a long way to go and no guarantee of help, returns to spur her into reluctant and agonising action.

Stand up. Lean on the bin for a second. Listen. Nothing obvious to worry about. Don't forget the beach bag. She really should have insisted Barry leave her the good little rucksack he'd ordered online from Canada. This bag is ridiculous. Oh well, nothing for it now. Just one foot in front of the other and she'll be at the hospital in no time. They'll be able to help her there. Of course they will.

***

THE MAN

He's almost at the main road when he hears them. The good news is they're not worried about being quiet - so they're clearly not on a hunting trip. The bad news? It sounds like there are several of them and they are angry and spoiling for a fight. He's not quite sure he trusts his senses in his weakened state, but his best guess from the acoustics is they're maybe twenty metres away, around the corner but heading his way.

He has a split second to decide, and not much longer before he's visible and sure to become the target of their currently unfocused rage.

He makes it back up the hill and across the road in maybe thirty long, awkward strides and half as many seconds. They're just rounding the corner as he launches himself headlong into the wild and overgrown hedge that was once the publican's pride and joy and bordered one of the areas best-loved beer gardens. By chance he's picked a thinner patch and his momentum takes him all the way through – but not without ripping the rucksack from his back. He's cut and bleeding from one cheek and the backs of his hands, but otherwise in one piece, as he lands on his shoulder and affects a roll to reduce any damage from the impact.

Barry would have appreciated that. Wanker.

His ankle is on fire and throbbing as if it's about to burst, but he can't hear any increased activity from the gang. Equally they haven't gone silent. Always a warning sign, that. He can see the rucksack on the other side of the hedge. He reaches out a long arm from his prone position on the turf to snag it and try to pull it back through – but he only manages to drag it half way into the bush before he's forced to stop, let the loose strap drop from his grip and shuffle back on his elbows in an awkward retreat.

Cigarette smokes wafts past him on the breeze, and for a second he's back in the beer garden. A cold pint of lager, some Scandi cider on ice for Lucy. Before the pregnancy. Before the miscarriage. Before Barry. At least he thinks before Barry. Before he knew about Barry anyway. Same thing.

The voices are almost on top of him now. One of them sounds vaguely familiar. Maybe one of the building committee members from the adjacent block - Adam something or other? He'd been one of the most awkward and annoying residents to deal with, a real stickler for all the pointless rules and regulations. No laundry on the balconies was his personal bête noir. Everyone must take their turn tending the communal garden was another he enforced with spreadsheets and pinned up lists and passive aggressive reminders. At least he'd ended up enjoying that one. He'd even taken Lucy's shifts - although Adam hadn't been too happy about that. Something about being outside and focused on tending the plants and bushes had been the escape from his job, and his life, that he'd never known he'd needed. If only he'd made as much of an effort with his marriage.

Adam is arguing with someone, a woman's voice, and then another of the gang gets involved. It sounds like Mr. Singh from the dry cleaners in the parade of shops with the jewellers. Lucy had liked him, maybe that was why he hadn't. He'd always resented the cost of dry cleaning, of repairs and alterations. They really should have been taught darning in school. Once he'd caught a toe in the seam and ripped open the cuff of his newly altered trousers. It had seemed like the end of the world in that split second. And he'd blamed Singh for it. Must have left it loose, by accident or on purpose.

That was one of the strange things about the post-Corona world, it was the same people as before - just fewer of them - but they were different. He had been one of the only ones not to turn to a bigger group for support, friendship, protection. He'd become a hermit, once more self-isolating for self-preservation, but this time not from the virus but from humanity. Or what was left of it. The gangs in his area weren't bikers or Albanian mafia or anything like that - they were either local residents and former business owners like this one, or just increasingly brazen and violent groups of the same disenfranchised youth that had existed before, the hoodies increasingly without a heart. So even the gangs were kind of divided along class lines. Classic Britain. Even at the end of the world the class system somehow still survives and thrives, like a post-apocalyptic moral cockroach.

It seems like the gang members have got over whatever the disagreement was and are settling down just on the other side of the hedge. Now what? He can't return to the main road, the quickest direct route down the hill to the hospital. And it feels too risky to try and wait them out with only a couple of feet of patchy foliage to hide his existence. So it has to be option three: detour.

He's about to try and grab the rucksack when he hears footsteps coming yet closer to his hiding place. He can just about make out the outline of Mr. Singh – for it is he, although something about him seems strange, different – as he stops on the pavement on the other side of the hedge, then bends down and yanks the rucksack out from the bush. Fuck. He freezes. Singh unzips the bag and rummages through it, grunting to himself as he does so, then zipping it closed again and looking up and almost directly at him. From the other side of the hedge he can see Singh's eyes sweeping the shrubbery, trying to decide if there's anyone there. He can't hold his breath much longer, and he can feel a cough tickling up in the back of his throat – but just when he's sure he's about to give himself away the former dry cleaner turns on his heels, raises the bag skywards in a triumphant salute and lets out a strangled war cry as he skips and careens back to the others with his loot secured.

***

1st January 2021

Today is New Year's Day. At least I think it is. I've not quite managed to keep up with regular diary entries and that's pretty much the only way I've been keeping track of the passage of time over the last few months. Sometimes I miss a few days, so I just guess how many and start the new entry from then. My last was what I think was Christmas Eve – and I figure it's been about a week since then.

Anyway, there weren't any fireworks to watch from the balcony last night. Although I did sit out there, on my own this time, and swig some vintage champagne – you remember the one Lucy, that your parents gave us to open when we next had something big to celebrate? I think they were hoping for a grandchild. Well, I opened it – to see in the first year "A.L.", "After Lucy".

Sitting out there in the cold, with only my plants for company, I got to thinking about what was important. I didn't come up with an answer. I know it's not "things" – almost all my material possessions have become obsolete. But I'm also not sure it's people. I think perhaps the world would be a better place if we all just lived alone, lived separate lives. Mankind as a community seems to have failed, if you ask me. The only 'communities' I see left are vicious, violent, selfish.

I feel like death today. I may have drunk too much of the champagne. And I definitely didn't eat enough, or stay hydrated enough, to avoid the effects of so much alcohol after so long without it. I might have to raid my store in the lock up garage for something suitable to eat on a hangover – perhaps there's a tin of baked beans with sausages in there. You'd never let me eat that.

***

THE DOCTOR

Where he can he takes the backstreets, and uses the gradient of the hills to freewheel for reduced engine noise. When he does so he can hear a gurgling and occasional cough from behind him. It doesn't take a genius, let alone a doctor, to know the kid is in a bad way.

Nearly back. All told he's only been gone an hour. He'll have to find room for the kid. Still, he'll either live or die but he'll be less complicated than the pregnant woman would have been. Assuming she ever even existed. How much longer could he carry on like this? At least the outside world contact had almost completely stopped - he hadn't had a call on that frequency for weeks before her voice cut through the static. Most of those who had known how to get hold of him were dead by now, which helped.

The kid coughed, a wet bubbling cough like a partially blocked drain. Not long now. He'll be back at the hospital and the kid will live or die. That's life. That's the power of the doctor. Sometimes anyway.

As he rolls past the deserted Denmark Hill station, the looming tower of the Salvation Army block, and its long-darkened neon crucifix, casts a shadow across the road. He sees a hunched form shuffling along the pavement. The brightly coloured beach bag is so incongruous he almost laughs. When was the last time anyone went on a trip to the seaside? The long hair gives no clues - the end of the world has been a great leveller for that, men and women alike all have long lank locks, or shaven heads. But the waddling gait is one he's familiar with - she's pregnant. Heavily. Ready to pop if he had to guess.

***

THE MAN

The second hedge, on the far side of the beer garden, had been more of a challenge. Wider, and more densely overgrown (maybe it was the southerly aspect), picking his way through it silently had been a painstaking and painful process. Shielding his face with his forearms had protected his eyes, but he was cut and scratched all over, and his clothes now look even more ragged than usual.

When he finally makes it out onto the other side he can see King's hospital, its central glass building gathering the cluster of old converted town houses and Victorian mansions that made up the rest of the campus to it like the pied piper. He stands and looks down the short stretch of road that leads to the main entrance - where in the distance the old wrought iron gates hang askance, bent and twisted, half off their hinges, as if they have been rammed by a tank. Between him and the hospital is an assault course of concrete bollards and burnt-out cars. He stands. He looks. The shadows lengthen imperceptibly. He's still standing when the birds - as uncaring of this abandoned scarecrow as ever - go quiet. Seconds later he hears the squeak and rattle of a vehicle wheeling along. He's not the only one. The gang too are in motion - he can just separate their hurried whispers and staccato footsteps from the growing sound of the whatever it is that this way comes.

As the ambulance rounds the corner the gang break cover - and the vehicle's engine coughs apologetically, ticks a few times and then finally roars into life. He catches a glimpse of a mess of unkempt hair in the passenger seat as it speeds past; Adam, Mr. Singh and a stocky human dynamo of a woman he doesn't recognise in hot, sweaty pursuit. As the vehicle straightens out of its fishtail and lines up with the distant hospital block Adam and the woman arc out to either side and then make their move – heads down, arms and legs pumping hard, they approach in a pincer movement, one on each side. Just as first the woman and then Adam get their hands on their respective side's door handle Mr.

Singh glances over his shoulder. The former dry cleaner skids to a halt, his eyes fixed on the unwanted observer.

He only now realizes what it was that was different about Singh. He's no longer wearing his turban. Long waves of dark hair instead crown his head like the mane of a black lion. For a second he's frozen, rooted to the spot, just staring at this new, wild Singh; at Adam and the woman hanging on to the half-open doors of the ambulance, their feet dragging along the road as they fight to stay upright. Then a woman's scream, strangely familiar, crashes into what he realises has been near-silence – and, the spell broken, he's off, haring back up and across the road on the diagonal, making a bee-line for the gate to the park. He nearly falls as his injured ankle threatens to give way, the ligaments screaming their silent protest at his sprint – and as he half-turns to avoid tumbling painfully to the floor he sees Singh in pursuit. Despite his injuries he reaches the gate, mercifully unlocked and ajar, several metres ahead.

It's been months since he was in this park, and without any maintenance it now looks wild and alien – the grass long, the bushes and hedges sprawling, the paths half-hidden. He follows the route of least resistance - the pattern of the undergrowth, the arc of the sun, subconsciously determining his course; a flight unchanged in millenia, a man escaping the hunt.

He can hear his pursuer huffing and puffing behind him like an impatient warthog but, zig-zagging through the rhododendrons and azaleas that have grown with wild abandon, he's able to keep out of sight and work his way deeper into the park. Somewhere way back behind him he hears a crash, what sounds like metal shearing and glass shattering, and one long, single drone from a horn.

Just when his ankle is about to finally give out on him he arrives, completely disorientated, at the old bandstand. The concrete is cracked, and weeds poke through everywhere, but the circular clearing means the only cover is the structure itself. He crouches on the far side of the pedestal and looks back from whence he came, eyes sweeping the almost unbroken wall of foliage opposite. He counts to a hundred, hardly breathing, as he listens for any sound of Singh. When he reaches a hundred he keeps on going, only finally stopping when he gets to a hundred and fourty nine and a ring-necked parakeet's sudden screech brings him out of his trance. No sign of Singh, the gang or the ambulance. It's darkening rapidly, the sun already dipping below the treeline that rings the bandstand clearing. Too late and too dangerous to try for the hospital today, he pushes on further into the park, keen to put a greater distance between him and the entrance in case they come back for him.

He's just about ready to lie in the dirt when a gate appears out of the gloaming - the dark metal, dulled by dust and dirt and half-concealed by a profusion of ivy, almost invisible in the half-light of the twilight park. The once-gold letters arcing overhead proclaim "Community Garden".

***

14th February 2021

It's incredible how fast the environment changed after everything went down. It was as if Nature was able to wrest back control of the planet from Man, to wipe the slate clean. Or at least that's how it seemed at first, over that long, cloudless summer when the pollution burned away and the sky seemed bluer than ever before. Now the weather seems intensified, erratic, capricious. It might just be that the damage we did tipped the balance permanently, and this is the result. But sometimes I wonder if it's her revenge, if it's Mother Earth (or whatever you want to call this complex symbiotic ecosystem) punishing us for our transgressions. It's as if the weather, the whole planet, has turned on us – is doing everything it can to make life for those of us who survived the outbreaks more painful, more difficult. Fair's fair, I suppose. The beneficiaries seem to be the plants and trees – the sun and the rain enabling them to grow faster and bigger than ever before. We're being rewilded, whether we like it or not. On balance, I think I like it. Let's go back.

Today's Valentine's Day by the way. Or at least it's the day I've decided is Valentine's Day. Having a diary has given me a way to control time – it makes me feel omnipotent, in control of my own reality. So, today is Valentine's Day, because I say today is Valentine's Day. After my experience on New Year's I am not going to drink (and I'm, not sure there's any alcohol left here anyway, those first few weeks after you left saw most of it polished off). I think I'll just sit on the balcony with the roses – they've been flourishing.

***

LUCY

She'd thought she'd run the whole gamut of emotions when he'd stopped to pick her up - fear, confusion, relief and then an intense, tearful and hormone-infused deep gratitude that made her cry so hard she could swear it triggered the next contraction. But this, this was another feeling yet again – abject terror. Fear for herself, but ten thousand times stronger – and for the first time – fear for the life of her unborn child. Her scream is one not only of terror but of anger and of defiance. The man hanging onto her now-open door almost loses his grip at her roar.

The ambulance lurches hard right, then jags back to the left as the driver regains the wheel – the sharp change of direction causing her to bang her head hard against the doorframe. She must have scared the shit out of him.

Poor man.

Wow, she hasn't thought those words in a long time! She feels the wet, warm trickle of blood breaking cover from her hairline and running unimpeded down her pale, dry skin. Her tongue darts out, she can't help herself, tasting the strange metallic tang as if for the first time.

She turns to the open door and realises she knows the man being dragged along with them. It's Adam - that jumped up busybody from the committee. His face is frozen in a terrifying rictus grin, an alien expression like a melted mask. He only ever seemed to tut and mutter and raise a single eyebrow – she'd always done her best to ignore it, but just thinking of it now makes her wish she had, just once, smashed his smug face into the wall of his beloved mansion block.

She hears a yelp from the man sat next to her and out of the corner of her eye sees a stocky woman clamber onto the driver's lap and headbutt him hard in the face. His grip adjusted, his feet now skimming the tarmac balletically, Adam emits a prehistoric growl, tenses his arms, springs from the road surface and launches himself. He's almost inside the vehicle when he disappears. A mist of fine red spray settles on her, unsettlingly warm. She realises the door is gone too, and cranes her neck out, back and round to see the door wrapped around a now-leaning lamppost, one half of Adam on either side.

She vomits in her mouth, and is still debating whether to swallow it down or not when a contraction hits her insides like a bear trap. She dribbles the bitter bile between gritted teeth. Then there's a bang. And dark nothingness.

***

THE DOCTOR

Everything hurts. Everything is black. He can't separate the noises out, there's definitely the muted, insistent drone of the ambulance's horn, but filtered through a ringing, hissing, popping that overlays everything. As the blackness begins to throb, and swirl with dark reds and painfully sharp yellows and greens, he can feel his nose is broken. Still not ready to open his eyes, his hands come up to his face and trace the now-crooked line of his badly deviated septum. His cheek burns, and from it he picks a hard chunk of something wet and sticky. Finally allowing one eye to open just a micrometre, he realises he's holding a human incisor between his forefinger and thumb.

Eyes now open, despite the painful throbbing that threatens to burst his skull, he surveys the carnage around him. The windshield is shattered, the short-haired woman now a bloody, crumpled lump of flesh and torn clothes twenty metres up the road, a smear of reddy-brown blood describing her journey across the tarmac. His pregnant passenger is no longer beside him. He feels a lurch of panic in the pit of his stomach.

He half falls out of the vehicle and, lying on the floor and gazing past the anti-terrorism concrete block that had brought the ambulance to an immediate and painful stop, sees a man helping the pregnant woman towards the hospital building. He scrambles to his knees, then claws his way upright using the folded bumper and concertinaed front end of the vehicle for support. But just as he's about to stagger after the pair a banging from behind him stops him in his tracks. The man is ushering the expectant woman – he really should have asked her name, but it all happened so fast – into the hospital. *His* hospital. They disappear within – and the banging, scraping sound from the rear of the ambulance reclaims his attention. The ringing in his ears and skull has retreated, although as he turns his head a wave of nausea accompanies a crescendo of hissing then a gentle pop. He can hear almost normally again. The trickle of blood from his ear goes unnoticed.

He'd almost forgotten about the lad in the back, but opening the rear doors he's slammed in the chest by the gurney as it, and the young man, slide into him. The kid's lost a lot of blood but he's somehow still conscious – alert enough to have almost kicked his way out. He rights the gurney, wipes some of the thick, foamy blood from the kid's mouth with his sleeve, listens for his breathing, checks his pupils, gives his hand a squeeze (the same hand that, he can't help but think, would have happily choked him to death in order to steal his ambulance and supplies) and gives the trolley a sharp shove to get it rolling in the direction of the hospital. He's already apprehensive about what he will now find there, his haven seemingly finally compromised, but if he's going to save this patient there's no other choice.

If only he'd never answered that distress call. Not the first time he's thought that. He's still never ignored one though. Old habits.

***

THE MAN

The tears just come. He sinks down onto the grass, head on the turf, as if he's found the direction of Mecca. His fingers seeking out, and then burying themselves in, the cool, dark loam. Once through the gate, reaching up to place his palms on the sign as he passed beneath those golden letters, he'd pushed through the tall grass and wild bushes and trees in an almost religious stupor, a fervour of hope and exhaustion that had brought him stumbling into the clearing and the discovery of this unexpected oasis.

He lets the emotions out, the teardrops bending the stalks of grass beneath his head and sliding off to disappear forever. When the tears no longer come, and his back begins to ache, he pushes himself up onto his knees – suddenly panicking that he might be being observed. He can't see anyone around, but this wondrous place is no accident. Someone has tended the garden – cut the grass, fed and watered the plants, cultivated the vegetable patch and fruit orchard. But also very deliberately let the perimeter grow wild – high and dense - keeping this haven hidden from prying eyes without.

Looking closer he picks up some clues that, piece by piece, indicate the mysterious gardener may no longer be in residence. Windfall apples, some of them on the turn, litter the ground. The compost heap - brown and dry. The otherwise immaculate flowerbeds showing just the first signs of weeds. Like a forensic pathologist he's able to date the likely time of departure – the garden was constantly maintained, then abruptly left untended, perhaps seven days ago.

Just above the line of the distant hedge on the far side of the garden he can see the edge of the helipad on the roof of King's College Hospital. Despite everything he's no closer to his destination that when he set out. His eye is drawn back down to a dull splash of green jutting out from the side of the long, low greenhouse. As he circles around, keeping the as-yet unexplored greenhouse and its grimy door in sight, the shape reveals itself to be a giant plastic rainwater butt.

He realises how thirsty he is. He's not had a drink in hours despite his exertions – and his supplies were all in the backpack. But when he reaches the barrel he discovers that, like so much of the world, it has long since been vandalized and a huge crack near the tap at the bottom has caused all the precious liquid to seep out and into what has become a giant muddy puddle around its base. The time for pride is long gone. The sky is bruising and darkening and, with no streetlights, it will be pitch black before long. He'll never make it to the hospital before morning. He kneels down and uses a cupped hand to skim a mouthful of water from the top of the puddle. It tastes exactly as it is – lukewarm, muddy and stale. Gritty particles of God knows what swirl around his teeth and irritate his throat as he swallows it down.

He looks up to see dark shapes flitting through the trees overhead. Low and darting, at first he thinks they must be bats – but as he looks closer realises they are in fact swallows. Or maybe swifts. Either way, he's pretty sure if they're hunting this low that means there's a low pressure front around, with the insects they feed on driven closer to the ground. Which could mean rain.

He's no sooner thought it than the sky spontaneously brightens for an instant, strange shadows cast ominously across the garden, as a sheet of solid lightning links the heavens and the earth and turns the tableau into a movie set. The hospital roof gleams in a cold, silver sheen for a split second – then darkens to the sound of an ancient drum. The thunder and lightning are so close together that the storm must be right above him.

He gingerly gets to his feet and, as the first heavy spatters of rain complete their long journey back to the soil, limps back to the open door and finally enters the greenhouse. What once would have been a warm and bright space is dark, damp and musty – the glass long since clouded by dust and dirt. His eyes struggle for purchase in the gloom – but a second burst of sheet lightning starkly reveals the interior. Like the garden it's clearly abandoned – but once more the clues remain that it was a refuge until not long ago. He just has time to take in the tiny plastic pots of green shoots and the few remaining straggly plants that have survived their abandonment before the dark returns once more. With no sign of human occupation he waits – and when next the lightning comes his eyes search for receptacles discarded on the tables and benches. One more sudden illumination is all he needs to plan his route – then he limps into the half-light to retrieve as many items as he can. He manages to fill his arms and pockets, and get back to the doorway, with only a couple of banged kneecaps and stubbed toes.

By now the rain is hammering on the greenhouse roof, and the amplified noise, like being inside a snare drum, is almost unbearable. Despite the aural assault, he forces himself to take the time to take off all his clothes within the greenhouse before he steps out into the storm, naked as the day he was born, carrying a motley collection of pots, pans, jars and mugs. He places them carefully, away from where the rainwater is already starting to sluice off the filthy angled roof of the greenhouse and instead on flat patches of grass or soil where he can gently press them into the ground, or sweep debris up beside them, to prevent them toppling over in the wind and rain. His work done, he finds a spot in the middle of the grass, stretches out his arms, and tilts his head back. Facing the heavens, eyes closed, he feels the rain wash across his face, pool in the lines of his upturned palms, run down his spine and his breastbone. His roar is a silent one, but no less violent than the drumming beat of the rain and the portentous snap, crack and rumble of the thunder and lightning.

***

3rd December 2020

It's been a few days since I wrote in here. I've been busy trying to consolidate my supplies and make myself as self-sufficient as possible. I'm not sure what the date is really, but a diary needs a date before every entry doesn't it? Otherwise it's not a diary, it's just some kind of self-indulgent journal.

Last night I dreamt for the first time in weeks. I wonder if you dream, wherever you are, Lucy? I'm still writing most of these entries as if I'm addressing you, as if you might read this one day. I'm not sure why. I guess even before this all happened you were almost the only person I really spoke to anyway. It just feels natural. Despite everything.

Anyway, I had a dream. Not like Martin Luther King – not a dream of a better future (although are we living that now? A world where Man has fallen and Nature is back in the ascendancy?), but a dream of the past. I'm not sure if it was a better past. Different, maybe. "The past is a foreign country, they do things differently there". How true. We were back on that Greek island, you remember the one, that last holiday before 'The Event' – before the virus changed our world and holidays became a thing of the past, of dreams. We were on a boat, on a day trip to another, even smaller, wilder, more beautiful island. The sun was shining. And then it wasn't. From nowhere it was obscured by thick, rolling, angry black clouds. The wind kicked up. White caps appeared on the waves that grew and grew and began to buffet the tiny vessel that suddenly seemed entirely inadequate for crossing this angry sea. I looked at you and you were entirely calm. And that terrified me. And then the storm passed, and when I turned back to the bench at the back of the boat you were gone. I knew you hadn't fallen overboard - you had just 'gone', you just no longer existed in this reality. I wasn't able to understand what emotion I felt at that exact moment, but then the sun broke out and I felt its warmth on my cold, wet skin and I closed my eyes and smiled. I had forgotten you in that moment, and I was happy.

When I awoke it was sadness, not happiness, I felt. And I wasn't sure if it was because you had gone, or because I had woken up.

***

PART TWO
CHAOS

LUCY

The room is so dark that she doesn't even realise her eyes are finally open until she's almost blinded by a bright light, as if a flare has detonated in the room. A second later the crack and rumble of the thunder enables her brain to make some semblance of sense of what's happening. Her eyes are open. The room is pitch black – but the windows are uncovered, and the violent electrical storm once more discharging outside throws her surroundings into stark relief. She's lying prone on a kind of reclining trolley, in the centre of a bare room. The linoleum floor and ceiling tiles, the walls lined with that very specific kind of cupboard, the smell even despite months of disuse, all tell her she's finally here. The hospital.

She'd dreamt of this moment. Dreams, and latterly nightmares. She'd never wanted kids. For the longest time she'd had no interest in motherhood. Then something changed. Not overnight. Not noticeably, at least not at first. A gentle, subtle mission creep until her objectives had turned around a hundred and eighty degrees. The realisation had been as terrifying as it was exhilarating. I want a baby. Let's make a baby. And they had. And as it grew and developed she'd imagined what it would be like to give birth – daydreamed that somehow she could remake the world and bring forth her child in a birthing pool in a hospital suite surrounded by totems of her life. But when her unborn child had been torn away from her she'd told herself that was it. As they grew apart it seemed like the best thing, like nature had known better and had saved them from a mistake. Or so she told herself. She acted numb. But she felt a loss, a pain and a yearning, that had never gone away. Then, when she realised that one of those final, painfully earnest couplings before she had walked out from their shared life in the flat had somehow planted the seed of a new life in her, when she knew there was no way back to the life she'd imagined before, she'd accepted that she needed to wrest back control of what lay ahead. That past life already jettisoned, she'd taken from her new lover - Barry - everything he could give her, and then she'd succeeded in making him leave. She didn't want to be the leaver, not this time. And then the dreams, and this time more often than not the nightmares, returned.

Darkness returns, her eyes unable to adjust immediately as the afterglow of the lightning dissipates. Then the shapes around her slowly solidify out of the gloom – the window frames, and the black outlines of the trees beyond swaying wildly in the wind, the counter top running around the room between low and high cupboards, the industrial style basin and washing area. A man. Her chest tightens. Definitely a man. There, in the corner where the walls, floor and ceiling converge. She relaxes a fraction as she remembers how she got here – the ambulance, the young doctor who took her in. She's about to thank him but realises she doesn't know his name. Before she can get out the words the lightning invades the room once more – and she can see, for certain, that it's not him.

"Hi Lucy".

"Hi Barry".

He looks different - still tall, but rangier. The same black 'combat' outfit he'd worn the day he left, his hair and beard fractionally longer but hardly those of a wildman - but something in his eyes, in the angles of his face, in the set of his shoulders, reminds her of a panther.

***

THE DOCTOR

The ambulance gurney almost slides out of his grasp as he manoeuvres it down the access ramp and out of the torrential rain, water sluicing past, soaking his feet to the ankles, sending sticks and leaves and the ancient, faded detritus of a world long gone spinning and whirling in miniature eddies. The kid on the trolley is soaking wet, pink rivulets of diluted blood running off him like meltwater down a glacier. He coughs and splutters as the rain fills his mouth and chokes him. They finally make it to the flat, dry concrete of the underground car park. The storm is raging outside but down here it's like being in a bunker – the lightning barely penetrates, the thunder and the hammering of the rain just a gentle background hiss.

He pauses, willing his senses to sharpen. His exhausted brain conjures from nowhere the image of a meerkat sentry, raised on hindlegs, alert to any danger – until the silent owl swoops in for the kill. It's been nearly a year since there was any television, but before things had disintegrated he'd loved to watch natural history documentaries. He'd identified with the predators, with their cunning, their survival instinct, with the finality of their hunt. He tunes out the muffled noise of the storm, the wheezing almost-death-rattle of the kid, the pounding of his own blood, and scans for intruders. No sign. He's pretty sure he saw them come in through the main entrance. If so, there should be no way he could have got in here. And no way up to the upper floors. *Should* be...

He knows the way by heart, wheeling the trolley expertly through the darkness without a single collision, right to the back of the lot – and the only route all the way up to the operational, and occupied, upper floors.

He bangs open the emergency doors with the trolley, ignoring the gurgling whimper of his patient. Time is of the essence.

There hasn't been an operational lift in the hospital building for nearly a year. As soon as it stopped working he knew he'd need a solution if he wanted to carry on bringing the sick and wounded up. Having moved all the supplies and equipment up to the top few floors he had been loath to even contemplate relocating not only all the gear but also his rag-tag collection of patients, gathered to him like moths to the flame, their navigational systems sent haywire.

He carefully collapses the legs of the ambulance's trolley, so the kid is only a few inches off the ground. Next, he attaches the top edge of the trolley, where the rail is smeared with blood and a few stray hairs, to a rope and pulley system that sits at the foot of the stairs. Here begins a series of sheets of metal and wooden planks that form a patchwork quilt of a ramp that spans half the width of the staircase and disappears around the corner out of sight. With the gurney now attached, he grabs one end of the rope and starts up the steps, dragging his patient up the makeshift ramp.

He's almost reached the first corner, the first switchback where the stairs form a landing before turning back on themselves, and thus the first potential resting point where the ramp becomes flat, when the rope starts to slip through his fingers. Lubricated by the not-yet-dry blood of his patient, that he hasn't even thought to wipe off, the cord is halfway from his grasp before he recovers – his hand snaking out and catching the final few inches of rope, arresting the descent of the trolley before it has enough momentum to break free completely. He wipes his other hand on his trousers and takes a firmer grip. He can feel the burn in his shoulders, his neck and his back. It's going to be a long haul to get this patient – this kid who would have happily slit his throat and stolen his ambulance, his supplies, his life – up to the top floor and the supplies and equipment that might, *might* save his life.

The next flight he takes slow and steady, concentrating on his breathing and his posture and not rushing despite the growing aches in his muscles. It's been a while since he had to haul anyone up like this. He's sure it was easier then. And this kid is *light*. He makes a mental note to try to eat a bit more, and work harder on his stretches and core strength exercises. The beginning of the outbreak, 'lockdown', should have been a clue, a pointer for things to come. Stuck indoors, muscles slowly atrophying, neck and back seizing and locking from poor posture and insufficient exercise. He'd never really recovered physically from those first six months of bad practice and poor self-care - despite his efforts to get in shape as society, and the hospital around him, collapsed.

He's just started up the next set of steps, which will finally take him above ground level and closer to his final destination, when he stops. Unable to hold the makeshift stretcher he gently releases his grip and allows gravity to slide it back down the last couple of metres until it sits back on the landing. The kid lies there motionless, the only sign of life the bubbles that appear in the frothy blood around his mouth and neck in time with the almost imperceptible rise and fall of his shattered chest.

There it is again. It sounds like a wolf. Or a hippo. Something in pain, or fear, or both. An undercurrent of anger perhaps. He only finally realises it's definitely human when he hears a second sound – deeper, half growl half bark, but in fact speaking words. A man. A man and a woman. Arguing. And then the wounded moan again. It's her. *The* woman. He's not an OB-GYN doctor, and he's not a father. In fact, he had always avoided even watching any documentaries about birth. He preferred to believe at least this one act held a little bit of beauty, of magic - and A&E and delivery ward programmes looked like they'd quickly burst that bubble. But now he can make sense of the sounds, can picture the scene beyond the emergency exit door before him, and those that will surely follow. Her labour has progressed, and she's arguing with the man – whoever it was he saw carrying her off...

The kid bleeding out on the stretcher forgotten, he steps forward, his fingertips reaching towards the 'push' bar that will open the door to a different future. He hesitates. He doesn't know these people. Doesn't owe them anything. And once he goes through this door he is potentially putting everything at risk. He can carry on up the ramp with his original patient or...

She's squatting down on her haunches as if she's using a longdrop toilet way out in the bush, facing the wall, in the far corner of the room. The man is turned away from her, and from him, staring off into the middle distance beyond the doors that lead back towards the corridor, the main entrance, the world of chaos and freedom beyond.

"For fuck's sake Lucy just" – and the words stick in the tall, black-clad man's throat as he turns to address the woman only to find a third party suddenly appeared in the room like Banquo's ghost – as bloody and portentous.

She too turns to him, as if she felt the atmosphere change, sensed his eyes on her. He's suddenly conscious of the myriad paths all their lives could take from this moment, sees their futures spider out from this present in silken threads that branch this way and that until their destinations become so multitudinous and disparate their very existence is called into doubt.

He notices that the man has not moved to protect the woman, but instead taken a step forward and readied himself on the balls of his feet. Remembering how he looks, blood-drenched and quite possibly wild-eyed, he's about to raise his hands in a universal gesture of supplication when she speaks the first words he's heard come from her mouth.

"It's you".

Both men pause.

"The guy from the ambulance".

He realises that even though she never spoke during their ninety second ride together, before the crash, he has indeed heard her voice before. He holds up a blood-smeared palm in modest hello.

***

THE MAN

He wakes with a crick in his neck, razorblades in his throat and the sudden realisation that it's daylight. The storm has passed. The day is old enough that the greenhouse is lit from without, despite the barnacle-like properties of the grime that no storm will ever shift.

As he rises, he's able to see a glimpse of the past within the glass walls – the ghosts of plants and trees, fruits and seeds, that once filled this place. Nothing conjures up any image of the man, or woman, who had maintained this sanctuary though – they remain hidden, the mere existence of the place the only clue to the kind of person they might have been. He realises he is thinking in the past tense. He can't help but assume they are dead. He doesn't correct himself. One way or another, they're gone.

Outside the containers that have stayed upright overnight, despite the storm, are now filled with fresh rainwater. He picks out stray leaves and twigs, the odd drowned insect, and allows himself a swig or two from the first few he gathers up. He holds the water in his mouth for as long as possible, willing it to absorb quicker, to bring the euphoria of genuine hydration. He's reminded of stories, he was never sure if they were urban legends or genuine facts, about how Native Americans (or was it Kenyan distance runners?) would keep a pebble in their mouth as they ran. He might even have been told about that on the survival weekend with the proto-Lucy.

Lucy.

He wipes the dribblings of the last swig of rainwater from his mouth with the back of his hand, sucks the droplets from his grubby fingertips and straightens his back, bringing the helipad and top floor windows of the hospital into view above the hedge line.

He sees a shape flit across one of the windows. Then a second, not far behind the first. They could be anyone. If they're even people. Still, he's come this far.

Before he sets out, he decants all the collected rainwater into the biggest vessel he can find and performs a circuit of the garden, sipping as he goes. On his foraging mission he finds a patch of wild garlic and carefully chews the leaves, washing them down with some more water to stop them burning his throat. Then, lo and behold, their bulbous green tops giving them away as they poke through the long grass, asparagus! He breaks the stems close to the ground and brings a stalk to his mouth, folding it in half in his hand as he does so. He chews it slowly, allowing what little saliva his body can muster the opportunity to break the tough fibres down. Finally, just when he's ready to give up and set off, he sees a flash of red half-hidden in the undergrowth. Carefully pushing the dangling branches of the overhanging bush away he uncovers a long, snaking Gordian knot of thorns bejewelled with a profusion of crimson – wild strawberries. The sweetness is almost too much to bear, and he has to force himself to stop eating and instead carefully pocket as many of the remaining fruits as he can into the most padded pocket of his coat. Precious cargo stowed, he takes a sighter of the hospital and disappears into the undergrowth.

As he pushes through the bushes, and out into the wildflower meadow beyond that was once a carefully tended park, he has what he can only make sense of as a waking out of body experience. He floats up above the park – and looks down at this tall, thin, straggly man limping through the waist high grass, his overcoat trailing behind him like a ragged cape or broken, torn wing. He laughs at himself - but not in a self-mocking, or self-loathing way. Instead, he laughs with surprise and a strange kind of joy. He may look pitiable but here he is – alive. He pictures the man he was, the man who sat alone at the campfire in a wet, cold wilderness wishing he could be anywhere else - even at home with Lucy. Except that wasn't what he had wished. He had wished he had the guts to talk to the female instructor. He can't even remember her name. He had wished Lucy had somehow stayed as she had been – wished that she was still like this better version of her, who was trying to teach him how to survive in a world he didn't recognise. A world without creature comforts. What had been the point? Now he knows. And now he laughs aloud at how far he has come. Alone.

He bangs his toe on a tree root, hidden in the long grass, and stumbles, his reverie dispelled. The food has energized both body and mind, and his focus returns to the task at hand: get to the hospital. But it's painful going. He's getting to the point where it's easier to list the parts of his body that aren't in pain. The wet grass wraps around his feet and legs and pulls insistently at his throbbing ankle as he struggles with every step to pull free.

***

7th March 2021

The thing that has really made a difference with my self-sufficiency is the plants. Sure, I've got a stash of long shelf-life items in the garage and I've been smart with my rainwater collections, but if it wasn't for the fresh fruit and greens I've been able to grow on the little balcony things might be very different. Plenty of sun, and something about the new weather since humanity's grip on the planet slipped, has helped them grow and flourish. It's certainly not my green fingers. Although they do say talking to your plants helps them grow – and that's something I do every day. And every night. They listen. And they give back, through their health-giving bounty. I thank each of them as I harvest what they have created and I'm always careful not to take too much, to leave them with enough energy to continue their joyous cycle, striving towards the heavens. They share my water, and I don't begrudge them it. Although they catch some rain if it blows in at an angle, like the blustery downpours we leaned into when we went up to Manchester and remembered why we had decided not to move up there, they don't get enough on their own. It feels almost spiritual sitting out there with them, all of us drinking slowly, regenerating.

I have withdrawn completely from everything else, but the plants keep me anchored. They remind me of a time before us. And that there will be a time after us. And by us I don't just mean me, or you, but all of us. All of this has opened my eyes to the fact that we will come to an end. Our cycle will finish. And, thanks to the outbreaks, that will be sooner rather than later. Soon enough to save this planet and those other organisms we share it with. At least that is my hope. So I water the plants, and I wait. They are my hope for the future.

***

LUCY

Barry is impatiently shuttling between taking the vanguard and bringing up the rear. As he waits on the landing above, she catches him staring at her bump, not for the first time. She's the slowest on the stairs. Slower even than the doctor dragging that poor kid on the stretcher. He seems to have gained a new lease of life, this stranger who answered her call and ended up with two patients for the price of one. Maybe it's Barry's presence – there's definitely some kind of weird alpha male, territorial pissing, fake-friendly stand-off going on. The doctor keeps refusing help – and he's pushing himself harder with every flight of stairs. She's not sure how long he can keep this up. Men are ridiculous. A sharp kick in her ribs catches her off guard and she leans against the wall for a second. Maybe she's having a boy. That'd figure.

As the doctor reaches the next landing he lets go of the rope and allows himself to sit down on the next step to catch his breath. Barry skips around him, nervous energy propelling him down the steps two at a time until he's immediately behind her. The kid gurgles incoherently. As the doc bends down to clear blood from his patient's airways, Barry whispers in her ear.

'Why didn't you tell me?'

She is about to reply when the doctor gets back to his feet and resumes hauling the stretcher up the ramp – causing Barry to bound back up the staircase to resume the lead. She's grateful, although part of her would rather have just had the guts to tell him there and then it's not his and that she doesn't want anything to do with him.

Before she can finish her train of thought another contraction hits and stops her in her tracks. She's really not sure she's going to make it to the top at this rate. She should have just had the baby in the empty emergency room, this is madness. It's going to come right here, right now, on the fucking staircase.

But it doesn't. The contraction somehow ends. At first, she's too dazed to even realise. When she does, she pushes Barry away (he's reappeared at her elbow again like an overattentive waiter) and starts putting one foot in front of the other again.

The climb goes on forever, the stairs and landings all alike, the only variety to be found in the materials used to fashion the jury-rigged ramp – corrugated iron, old doors, planks of wood, even a flattened cardboard box lain atop a taught length of what appears to be a tennis net, perhaps scavenged from the local public courts in the nearby park. The doctor stops to rest at almost every landing now – and she uses these moments to take short breaks herself. If she's not fighting a contraction, eyes screwed shut in pain, she tries to regulate her breathing while staring out of one of the corridor windows. She sees him stop again, the young man on the stretcher pale and seemingly lifeless. The rain has finally stopped, and she watches as the dawn breaks over the sodden landscape beyond. Movement in the grassy expanse below draws her eye but the dark shape, it looks almost like a giant crow, is gone again before she can properly focus.

There's something out there, in the park.

She resumes her march to the summit. As the doc and his deathlike patient rest on the final landing before the top, Barry slowly slinks down the stairs towards where she is once more leaning against the wall, breathing her way through another contraction and cursing them all under her breath. He's noticeably more circumspect, this time he seems more like a hyena, circling out of range and keen to nip at her haunches - but wary of a fatal kick. She wishes she had the snarl, the animal rage or even the physical capability, to show him not to mess with her right now – but she can only whimper as he takes her arm and lays it across his shoulders, helping her upright and guiding her step by step to the final door above.

***

THE DOCTOR

He can tell there's something between them, but whatever it is seems at the very least messy and complicated, and at the worst downright dangerous. Something about the guy, Barry, keeps tripping his internal early warning system. At least they finally all made it up those damn stairs. Felt like it took all night. In fact, it pretty much did.

His patient is still alive. Just. And his other patient has managed her contractions like a true yogi, and might have bought them enough time to at least attempt to deliver this baby in a room instead of on a staircase. First, he needs to get some blood (plasma might be the technical term?) into this kid before his blood loss becomes so critical there's no coming back from it.

He drags the stretcher over to an empty bed but doesn't bother trying to lift the lad onto it. Instead, he pulls the drip stand out from behind the bed and leaves it next to his young charge.

Blood.

Where did he stash the last of the blood? He'd managed to eke out his supplies until now. Just as well. The portable freezers he'd dragged up from the other floors had been the biggest drain on his generator – but without keeping them on, and cold, all his most precious supplies would have long perished. Syphoning petrol for the jenny was one of the riskiest tasks he undertook, and he'd had to travel further and further from the hospital to find abandoned cars that had anything left in the tank – heading out alone and on foot into the dark and, if he was lucky, returning laden down with cans of petrol or diesel, or very occasionally both, for the generators and the ambulance.

It's ominously silent. He's standing in front of the last remaining freezer and there's no tell-tale rattle and hum from the compressor. He can barely bring himself to open the door, wishes he was religious enough for a quick Sign of the Cross to be anything more than a cynical last resort. When he does finally pull the freezer open the light fails to turn on.

Fuck.

Now that he comes to think of it, he should be hearing the noise of the generator too. This is really not good. Ok, first things first. The freezer unit is off but, reaching inside, his hand registers the cool of the interior. His fingers find the last remaining bags of blood plasma – and they're still icy to the touch. Maybe not -30°c but hopefully not too far off. Yet. The generator can't have been off for long.

He closes the door as fast as he can, desperate to keep the warm air out and trap the cold air in. Turning his attention to the root of the problem he discovers that not only is the generator is off – it won't restart. A quick investigation reveals the problem. The petrol has run out. He must have forgotten to check before he left to answer the pregnant woman's call. He knows he doesn't have any more in the building, and the ambulance runs on diesel. The plasma might still be useable, but he'll surely need both packs if he's to save the kid – and one will have to stay in the freezer until he needs it. So he really needs that generator up and running again, stat.

First things first. He grabs one of the cold bags of blood and runs for the door. Crashing through it, shoulder first, body on the half turn to cradle the bag of life-giving crimson, it takes a second for him to see that Barry and Lucy are no longer there. No time to ponder. He skids to a halt on the once-polished floor beside the stretcher and hooks up the bag to the drip. As he watches the red leading edge of the blood curve down the clear tubing he enters a reverie, exhausted by the events of the last 24 hours and entranced by the progress of this tiny crimson tide and the potential it holds.

He stands in a three-piece suit, cradling a baby in his arms. It looks up at him and smiles. The sun is streaming in through the bay window. In the distance a church bell chimes. On the final tolling of the bell the scene dissolves, and he's back in the hospital. He stands over the bed where Lucy lies, impossibly beautiful, the drip delivering its stream of blood to keep her alive. She is his. He is not alone. And then, as soon as he thinks it, he is. Alone. And back in the room – the real room this time. The drip remains, but his patient is a punk kid – a gang member who tried to carjack him for his ambulance. And Lucy is nowhere to be seen.

***

LUCY

She hates that she's grateful, but she is. Grateful she's not alone – even if it's Barry (*after all this it's fucking Barry*!) who is there with her. Soon after the doctor – Sanjay he'd told her to call him – had disappeared in a hurry, muttering about blood and freezers, she'd felt something she'd somehow known, deep down in her primaeval core, was different. This was it. It was coming.

She'd wandered off on her own, pacing and breathing and trying to keep what little she felt she had left of herself together. Barry had come to find her. And now here she is, lying on a bare hospital bed, in an empty room, a human sacrifice surely no god would want. Barry's scrabbling around somewhere, trying to unearth some more of Sanjay's hidden stash of medical supplies. She can just about make out the creaks and slams as he tries each cupboard in turn, the muttered expletives under his breath. Christ, she hadn't missed those. Even now, with her cervix dilating at a rate of knots, it's still like fingernails on a chalkboard hearing him curse like an angry old man.

The scuffed, irregular footsteps of his loping gait approach, his shadow falling across her face from where he stops and stands behind the bed, out of sight.

"Lucy".

She forces herself not to look, not to crane her neck to try and meet his gaze. She can imagine what his eyes are like right now. He'd always tended to the manic, although it had taken some time to reveal itself to her. The longer they had been together the worse it had got. And she'd already seen that it was worse than ever now, revealed in his furtive glances, piercing stares and skittish behaviours. He'd been on edge since the moment she regained consciousness enough to find it was him, however improbably, dragging her from the wreck of the ambulance and into the hospital.

She realises she hasn't answered, but before she can speak she hears the groan of an underused door swinging open and shut. Tilting her head back as far as she can she sees the upside down exit sign beyond her shoulder, the set of double doors coming to rest once more. No Barry.

Another contraction envelops her being, its only mercy the eradication of any worries about her erratic former lover. The eradication of *every* worry – except *how the hell am I going to survive this single moment.*

As it subsides, she prays for Sanjay, that his will be the next face she sees. He has kind eyes. She's caught his concerned glances at her. And although the hospital set up is halfway to madness she's got a feeling he's a good doctor.

I wonder where he keeps his other patients?

***

THE DOCTOR

He's weighing up if he has time to make a run for some petrol, to restart the generator before the last blood pack spoils, when the door slamming open behind him makes him jump.

"Lucy!"

But no, it's Barry - the restless, prowling carnivore with the wild eyes and the insincere smile. Something about his presence now, in the hospital – *his* hospital – brings to mind a different beast, a cuckoo in the nest.

He needs to go.

"She needs you."

"Where is she?"

"Down the main corridor, second door on the left."

He starts for the door, pausing on the threshold but not turning his head to look back at Barry.

"I need petrol. *We* need petrol. The last jenny is dry, without it she won't make it."

It comes out so easily, the whitest of lies. Just another small untruth paving his way.

"I'll go."

***

THE MAN

The sun is back to its pre-downpour strength, another painfully hot day building, inconsiderate of his pathetic condition. He stops in the shade of a straggly paper birch to rest his ankle. Absentmindedly picking at the loose bark, he stares up at the hospital, trying to find the window where he caught sight of them – the people. The bark peels away in a single, long, satisfying sheet - white on one side, a beautiful light brown on the other.

He can feel the need to urinate building. His bladder was weak before what became known as 'lockdown' – but something about his diet and fluid intake during the ensuing months of increasingly extreme privation had exacerbated the problem. Kidneys probably. Better to go now, micturate (he smiles at the lawyerly sounding word, an echo of the flowery prose he favoured before The Event) in the comfort of the shade rather than hobble on needing to pee. It's like anything – eating, drinking, sleeping – you should do it when you can in these situations.

But as he fumbles with his overcoat, and the awkward zip of his fly, his overworked ankle gives way and he's once more toppling to the ground. No controlled fall this time. Instead he keels over sharply, hands still trapped at his waist, head and shoulder banging the ground. As he lies there for a second, too weak and dispirited to do anything but allow his eyes to pull focus on the leaves of the birch high above him, he feels a seeping wetness and a warm stickiness combine around his thighs. It takes a moment to realise he hasn't soiled himself. This is worse.

When he stands the plastic measuring beaker of water is cracked and empty, its former contents now combined with the crushed pulp of a handful of wild strawberries and congealing, sticking his coat to his trousers. Suddenly he's not just in need of a pee but also thirstier than he's felt in hours, the wild garlic repeating on his breath. He pisses into the beaker, fully intending to reuse some of his own bodily fluids but, even as the amber, frothy liquid leaks away through the crack just a few centimetres from the base of the beaker, the overpowering smell of asparagus turns his stomach.

It already feels like a lifetime ago that he was practically hermetically sealed in his top floor flat. Everything in its place. A system. Just him and his plants. And Mr Tibbles of course. Simpler than when it had been the two – well, three - of them. Lucy hated asparagus – had always made a point of mocking him if, when he had somehow snuck it into the recipe, she went into their tiny bathroom after he had been for a pee. That was a different lifetime – a global catastrophe, The Event, creating a fork in the road, setting them on divergent paths. Whether or not it was better when she was there or not, there was no going back now. The flat, that life – either alone or with Lucy – was gone.

Get to the hospital.

That was his only goal now. He'd lived for so long without any longer-term plan than collecting rainwater or scavenging supplies that it felt like the synapses in his brain would now refuse to transmit any data that had even a whiff of a long-term future.

Don't fight it. Survive. Get to the hospital.

***

19th March 2021

My stomach is killing me. Not literally, at least I hope not – although who knows what state it's in, wouldn't surprise me if there's an ulcer in there fit to burst and free me from this existence at last. No, it's just cramping hard. Can't say I blame it.

The last few days have been nothing but rainwater and a tin or two of cream of tomato soup. Remember how often we ate that when we were desperately trying to save money, still thinking we could cobble together enough cash to afford a deposit to get us out of this tiny flat and into a nice big house ready for the arrival of our first child? Fate is a cruel mistress indeed. I'm sorry. I don't think I ever actually said it back then. Left it unsaid. Like so many things.

So, after nothing but sips of water and half cans of soup (I've been letting the plants rest and recuperate) I risked a little saunter around the block today, more to clear my head and stretch my legs than anything. I'd not seen any sign of gang activity in a while so it seemed as safe as it would ever be. And the weather was perfect – cool and clear but not too bright, no rain, no violent gusts of wind. Calm. Just what I needed.

I was still in the gardens of the estate when I heard an altercation on the other side of the hedge. I was able to push through to a point where I could observe without being seen. It was them, the gang. And they'd accosted some poor soul who was out scavenging on his own. He tried to escape, and they chased him down and pinned him to the road. But not before I saw him toss something into the hedge twenty metres or so up the hill from my hiding place. I knew it must be something important, something valuable. None of the gang seemed to have noticed. So I hunched down and waited. They took their time beating him, but I just kept my eyes trained on the spot where the item he'd tossed had vanished. I knew if I looked away I'd struggle to find the place again. Eventually they got bored, or tired, or both, and they grabbed his bag and took his boots and wandered off. I could hear a groan or two and a gurgle and then a long, slow breath that faded away into silence. Only then did I creep forward through the undergrowth, my eyes trained on the dark earth and deep green leaves. And there it was. An entire family size bar of dairy milk chocolate. I swear I heard angels sing.

I ate it all right there, squatting in the cool darkness of the bushes.

And now I have a stomach-ache.

***

LUCY

Since Barry disappeared, she's felt herself slipping away. Getting weaker and more delirious as her exertions take their toll, and getting increasingly terrified with every second she lies there alone as a living creature attempts to make its way out of her body. She fantasizes about the appearance of her knight in shining armour, Dr. Sanjay.

She is in an eerie no man's land – a version of the Somme in South East London – mud and mortar fire, barbed wire and potholed roads and terraced housing. Sir Sanjay appears over the horizon, stood atop a brilliant white charger, clad in a battered suit of armour, riding to her rescue. He scoops her up from the mud and blood, his arms encircling her as he holds the reins. The horse stumbles on the debris of the battlefield. It falls, trapping her beneath its huge weight. It is Barry who somehow pulls her free. As he carries her away from the carnage towards an impossibly modern and pristine building, she turns back to see the good doctor unholster a pistol and apply the coup de grâce to the white horse's temple.

The sound of the doors swinging open brings her back to herself. She tries to regain a modicum of calm. She doesn't want to give Barry the satisfaction of seeing how out of it she is, how much she needs someone to tell her-

"It's alright Lucy. I'm here."

It's like a drug hitting her veins – the calming, reassuring voice of the doctor in her ear. She screams with the pain of another contraction. Her attempt to apologize fails, her "sorry" overpowered by the need to breathe and pant like a dog on heat.

***

THE MAN

He's close now, almost in the blissfully cool shadow of the hospital block. He crouches at the very edge of the park, peering through the low metal fence from the undergrowth. Just short of the main entrance it looks like a bomb has gone off. The ambulance is wrecked, listing in a pool of oil and shards of broken glass, plastic and metal, its front end folded around a massive block of concrete left in the road to do just that – stop vehicles in their tracks. At the base of a partially toppled lamppost he can see one of the ambulance doors, metres from the vehicle. A pair of feet protrudes from one end of the door. No man is tall enough for those to be his feet if the hands and arms he can see on the far side of the lamppost also belong to him. And yet they are. All four limbs belong to the same unfortunate - Adam, that prat from the housing committee. He recognizes the appallingly old-before-his-time 'fashion' sense, the cable knit cardigan and brown deck shoes now separated by several metres.

On the far side of the ambulance a dark brown smear on the road leads his eye to a second body. A crow is pecking at the back of the woman's head, its beak coming away wet, shining in the bright sunlight. It's about to peck again when it stops. Its head cocked, it waits. He hears a click, and the bird takes off, the flapping of its wings so painfully loud he fancies he feels the gusts of wind from where he hides.

The ambulance door slowly opens and a backpack, *his* backpack, reverses out. Singh slides into a sitting position on the tarmac, keeping himself hidden from the hospital beyond as he leans back against the tyre to inspect the items he has 'liberated' from the emergency vehicle.

He edges along the park perimeter, staying at least one layer of foliage from the road, bringing the ambulance, and the hospital, closer with every slow, careful step. When he reaches the limits of the park he crouches once more. As he watches he sees Singh take off the backpack, unzip it and bring out the diary. He's about to charge, swollen ankle and danger of discovery be damned, when he sees his intended target drop the book, and the bag, and roll onto his front. Singh is peering under the ambulance, his gaze trained on the hospital.

The man that comes out into the dazzlingly bright daylight moves like an insect, abruptly stopping and starting and changing direction. Something about him seems familiar but, before he can dwell on it, he sees Singh commando roll to the back of the ambulance, clamber into a crouch and peer around the corner of the vehicle. The former dry cleaner's prey is inching closer to him, the angular man scurrying from cover to cover unaware he is observed by not just one but two pairs of eyes.

As the man approaches, moving in and out of the long, jagged shadows cast by the unforgiving sun, more details become visible. The colour of his hair, the set of his jaw, the practical but entirely joyless survivalist's wardrobe. Barry.

He sees Singh cock back his right arm, raising what looks like a large mechanic's spanner behind his head, as Barry breaks into a low crouching run, one arm swinging a jerry can that skims back and forth above the road. Singh is rocking on the balls of his feet, readying himself to strike. He watches. It would be so easy just to wait, let it play out...

He's on Singh before he knows what's hit him. Like a nightmarish, vengeful scarecrow, running hard out of the park shadows with his long overcoat flapping, he envelops Singh and tackles him to the ground. Pinning his target's right arm to the road with one hand, smashing into his face with his opposite forearm, he follows through to grab and twist the metal tool from his grasp. A sharp blow to the temple with the spanner ends the dry cleaner's resistance. A dot of blood appears, welling up in a gentle spring before succumbing to gravity and trickling to his dark hairline, where it mingles with the wild tangle of ringlets like a woodland stream disappearing amongst the trees.

He rolls off the man and, lying prone, turns to look under the ambulance. Barry is kneeling on the far side of the vehicle, the petrol can on the ground beside him. He gets up, the spanner clenched tightly, and walks slowly towards the only man he's ever fantasized about bludgeoning into a sticky, bloody pulp.

Barry chokes, dark, pungent liquid spilling from his mouth, the hosepipe falling to the road. When he's recovered sufficiently, he spits, and wipes the corner of his mouth with his sleeve.

"Fuck."

"Hi Barry."

"It's diesel."

"What?"

"We need petrol."

"What?"

"We need petrol. Lucy *needs* petrol."

"Lucy's here?"

He'd known it. He was right. ***Get to the hospital.***

"We need the generator running, or she won't..."

"Won't what?"

"Make it."

When he steps forward Barry flinches. The strange, visceral, almost transcendental elation he feels dissipates when he realizes he is still wielding the spanner above his head. He lowers the weapon and holds out his other hand. Barry takes it, hauling himself up – and swiping him flush across the back of the head with the jerry can. Everything turns red, and he feels the terror of believing he is bleeding through his eyes, before everything in turn becomes green and his brain struggles to make sense of what is happening to him. Eventually all he can do is fall to his knees as his monochromatic vision gives way to total darkness.

***

25th November 2020

The worst thing about this new existence, worse than the deprivation, the hunger and thirst and struggle to survive, the dangers, the fear, the loneliness, worse than all of those is having too much time to think. Hell isn't other people. We can shut other people out, avoid them, ignore them, banish them... Hell is ourselves. Hell is being alone with nothing but your own thoughts - your regrets, your pain, your mistakes, the reality you have constructed for yourself. We are all prisoners of our choices. That is our real fate.

When I'm out scavenging for supplies my senses are heightened and my past vanishes to be replaced by the urgent immediacy of the present. Nothing else matters. I hunt for stores that have been missed by the gangs, caches that haven't been ransacked – and I put all my energies into moving silently, invisibly, safely. When I am on the balcony I can focus on the plants, in the garage I concentrate on taking stock of my supplies. But when I am inside alone, or even worse lying down trying to sleep (as I am now, or was until I picked up this stub of pencil and this self-indulgent diary), the demons rise up – the bad decisions, the missed opportunities, the things left unsaid. And I'm slowly coming to the realization that I have no weapon with which to slay them. I am powerless.

I don't blame you for Barry. I don't even blame Barry for Barry. How can I blame you for being brave enough to try and find some happiness elsewhere? I wasn't brave enough to do it myself. Perhaps I should have done. She wasn't you, that woman who ran my survival course. But perhaps that should have been the point. Barry's not me, after all. He's still a twat though. Just a different kind of twat (to me). Sometimes, like tonight, I think about the irony that we both went on those stupid courses – and that you found a way out through yours and I just found a way deeper into the mire. Falling for your instructor – I mean seriously, for one of us to do it would be careless, but both of us? Just as well I was too pathetic to do anything, or we'd be the butt of dinner table jokes for the rest of the millennium. "Did you hear about the couple that left each other for their wilder-

ness instructors?" Just as well there aren't any dinner parties anymore either.

***

THE DOCTOR

It's fortunate this is her first child. Less so for her, but it's certainly helping him. The labour is progressing slowly, it seems like she's hardly dilated at all, and he has time to leave her temporarily to check the drip is still replenishing his young attacker's blood supply. When he returns, she begs him to deliver the baby, but based on a quick inspection of her cervix he's pretty sure she still has a way to go. He can tell she's about to launch into a foul-mouthed rant, as soon as she gets her breath back, but he's spared her ire by the return of Barry.

"There you are. I got some. Petrol. Come on, what are you waiting for man!"

Barry, a half-crazed maelstrom in quick-dry clothing, has no sooner burst through the doors and waved the jerry can in their general direction, great glugs of the valuable liquid spilling onto the once-white floor, than he has turned on his heels and bounded back out again, barking over his shoulder for the doctor to hurry.

He pats her hand and forces a smile. Her smile too is an effort, but that seems to him more due to pain and exhaustion than insincerity. He feels a frisson of something he's not experienced for years.

"Fucking hurry up Doc!" bellows into the room. He blinks, turns, and leaves.

He can feel it all unravelling. He didn't expect Barry to make it back. But there could be a way to turn this back to his advantage. He just needs to manoeuvre the pieces correctly – and invisibly - once more. And Lucy. Yes, that is certainly an interesting development.

He catches up to Barry at the freezer, finds him sat on the floor beside the petrol can, rocking impatiently, his hands clasped across his knees. He snatches up the can, and marches past him to where the generator sits silent. He sniffs the can – definitely petrol not diesel. He could have sworn Barry would have gone to the ambulance. Maybe he's smarter than he gave him credit for. He better be careful. He pours some of the viscous contents into the machine, takes a step back, kneels down, closes his eyes and presses the ignition. Nothing.

Fuck, fuckity fuck.

A rustle of clothing, the squeak of a shoe on the linoleum floor and the audible pop of an overworked joint or two tell him Barry has stood up. He can't let him know the situation. This is mission critical.

He strides out from behind the freezer, his face as disarming a smiling mask as he can muster.

"Good news!"

"Why can't I hear it?"

"Oh, you will in a second, don't worry."

He can tell Barry hasn't quite bought the lie – and, lo and behold, he stalks past him to check the generator for himself. With Barry's back turned he ducks down, opens the freezer and pulls out a plastic package. Tearing it open he removes the syringe, pops the cap with his teeth and darts after him.

Barry is caught in a kinetic no man's land - half-stood, half-crouched and on the quarter turn – as he eases the needle into his exposed neck and presses down the plunger.

No going back now.

***

THE MAN

He comes to on the hot concrete, the strength of the sun sending colourful phantoms dancing across the black-red backdrop of the inside of his eyelids like projections on a theatre curtain. If his migraine was a cranial atom bomb, then this is total supernova. He opens his eyes, vomits a thimbleful of sharp, sour liquid onto the ground, and closes them again.

Lucy... Barry... Singh... Shit, Singh.

He forces himself to his feet, the spanner a red-tainted pendulum held at his side. As he staggers around the corner of the ambulance he swings it back above his head, ready to strike.

It clatters on the ground. Before him lies Singh. He hasn't moved. His hair fans out on the concrete like a rare coral, or the tentacles of a beautiful but deadly jellyfish – its natural darkness offset by the reflective gleam of wet blood. Something about the shape of the man's skull looks odd, like he's looking at it through a cracked mirror, the lines and angles no longer aligned. He sees himself in that mirror. His hands instinctively move to where there was once long hair, then fumble until they eventually find the newly-cropped nape of his neck.

No more Singh. No sign of Barry. Just get to the hospital.

The headache is so bad he can barely walk, and the brightness is so overpowering that it pains him to keep his eyes open. So he adopts a technique he'd practiced at home in the dark – only opening his eyes for a split second every ten steps, to quickly squint ahead and check for obstacles. It had started as a way to stop himself waking up too much on his worryingly regular middle-of-the-night trips to the toilet and then, when the proverbial shit hit the metaphorical fan, he had started adopting it as a training routine – testing himself on routes in and out of his flat and the building, seeing how far he could get without looking, or bumping into something. Making sure if he was blindfolded, or blinded, or operating in total darkness, he could still find his way to and from his refuge. He'd seen an old samurai movie that had given him the idea. Now, a spanner in place of a disguised cane sword, he shuffles through the debris between the ambulance and the hospital. He tries to focus his hearing, conscious of how exposed he is.

Slow your breathing, power down your unnecessary senses, home in on those you need.

As he walks, he hears something trapped in the sole of his shoe - a small stone, or possibly a cube of windshield glass - scraping on the road surface. Even with his eyes closed he can sense a shadow flit across his path – the slow beating of wings perhaps ten feet above his head suggesting a larger bird. A crow or a raven perhaps, or even a kite or buzzard – the birds of prey becoming an increasing part of life (and death) in London as their territories gradually increased. In his head he's Gary Cooper, this his long walk through the shadows of his own personal high noon. It helps him to cast himself as the hero. No one else had. Or would. And with good reason. But we're all the heroes of our own story, right?

Get to the hospital. Get to Lucy.

Nine.

He senses the temperature drop a fraction of a degree, the intensity of the bright light beyond his eyelids reducing noticeably.

Ten.

He opens his eyes. He is standing in the shadow of the hospital. It seems squatter, more squalid, up close. No longer the gleaming tower he'd been focused on since he set out but now somehow toadlike. The ramp down to the subterranean car park leads away to his left like the lolling tongue and gaping maw of a mythical beast from Japanese folklore.

He hears an engine in the distance, the sound making its way to him via a pinball table of surfaces. He just has time to limp into the darkness of the car park before the bin lorry trundles around the corner and stutters to an ungainly stop beside the ambulance. He recognises the man who is expelled from the passenger side door as another of the gang – can still picture him kicking at the shards of pottery on the access road, trampling leaf and stem beneath his worn-out biker boots.

When he sees the man find Singh, fall to his knees, and cry great hulking sobs into his motionless chest he turns away and walks slowly down the ramp into the darkness.

At the bottom of the ramp, he picks his way through an inverted archipelago of receding islands of rainwater run-off, and over a high-water mark deposit of sticks and other detritus, the last signs of the overnight deluge. The cool gloom of the car park rejuvenates him. As if bathing in an enchanted pool, he can feel his headache receding, his stiff and aching joints and muscles eased by the healing atmosphere. No longer needing to constantly close his eyes, he makes swift progress through the maze of cars and empty spaces. Keeping the letterbox of light that is the entry ramp behind him, he steers his course for the door at the back corner, above which a small metal box once housed a bright green man running for the stairs.

As his eyes adjust and his vision sharpens, he spots a trail in the dust, a pair of lines in the dirt where something has been wheeled through, wet enough to still be visible. Alongside the tracks intermittent spatters of blood, not yet dry, mark the margins of the route. He stumbles, finding just enough momentum to careen to the nearest car and use its bonnet to catch his fall. The bang as his palms dent the metal echoes ominously.

He can't get Barry's words out of his mind.

Lucy is here. Bleeding. Dying. With only that psychotic prick for company.

***

1st April 2021

I'm not sure if this date is even close to correct, but it feels oddly pertinent so I'm sticking with it. April Fool's Day. A big hello from me, your April Fool, dear reader. I've written a lot of these diary entries as addressed to Lucy, who you will have gathered was my wife but left more for a twat called Barry who was her survival instructor on one of those god-awful work team building away weekends. Well, no more. The chance that she will ever read this is so infinitesimally small it seems completely ludicrous to maintain the charade. Perhaps it was therapy to begin with. Now it just smacks of egotistical self-indulgence. If you're reading this, forgive me.

I have left no real mark on this world. My job didn't change anything, didn't make anyone's life better (including my own). I have no children. No legacy. Nothing to stand the test of time and contribute to the sum of human learning or even to the healing of this damaged planet.

So, this diary will have to do. A record of my experience in this fractured world. I actually hope no one reads it. I hope this, The Event, is actually the death knell for humanity. We have been living on borrowed time for a century or more. War, famine, pollution, poverty, cruelty. When does a species know it is beaten? Know it should just give up? That, on balance, it's a force for bad rather than good?

I have been a fool. We have all been fools, or worse. Let this be the last time.

***

THE DOCTOR

He checks the familiar restraints one more time. He should have a bit longer before Barry regains consciousness, but you can't be too careful. Satisfied he's secure, he wheels the bed with a practiced grace and speed through the corridors. A final push from his fingertips sends it freewheeling through the double doors like a drunk ejected from a saloon. He smiles before following.

The kid looks rough. He checks for a pulse. Weak, but there. Tough little blighter. The pack of plasma is almost gone. The one remaining pack in the freezer will be spoiled by now. This really is the last roll of the dice.

In seconds he has Barry hooked up, the blood flowing as fast as he can make it, through pristine tubing into a brand-new sack - chivvied along by his manual flexing of his unconscious patient's muscles.

He stands back to survey his handiwork, to gaze over his kingdom.

Look on my works, ye Mighty, and despair!

The circle of blood, flowing from one man and into another. Taking strength, bestowing life. This must be what it feels like to be a rain god.

Well, let it rain!

With the transfusions under control there's really only one place he should be – with Lucy, delivering the baby. Once again, giving life. He could get used to this.

He strides purposefully out of the room, the men already forgotten.

When he finds her, he can tell it's time. She looks exhausted. And scared. As if she knows.

"Don't worry. I've done loads of these. Before."

"Before?"

And then he remembers she doesn't know, can't know.

"Before all this."

His sweeping gesture needs no explanation. Before the world went to shit. He sees her relax. Well, as much as it's possible to relax in her situation. A softening of the eyes - the gentle wrinkling of the lines at their corners that are on their way to becoming full-blown crow's feet. He's always been preternaturally perceptive. A curse as much as a boon.

The rest is confidence. Project it. Instil it in her. Be calm. Be deliberate. Be a doctor. She doesn't know. She'll never know.

"Let's deliver this baby then Lucy – it's time for you to become a mum!"

***

LUCY

She can feel the calmness radiating from him. His eyes harbour a hypnotic intensity, so far removed from the 'anywhere but here' look that became the default subtext in the faraway gaze of her ex-husband, or indeed from the manic, flitting glares of her lover that nevertheless really boiled down to the self-same thing. She tries to anchor herself, last thing she needs is a man and his eyes. Now, or ever. She hopes it's a girl. Now is the time for a matriarchy to rise from the ashes of this shit-heap world. The women had shown the way – shown how it could be combatted, but the most powerful countries, the most powerful interests, and industries and corporations, were all run by men. And, sure as piss on a toilet seat, they'd flushed the globe down the pan for their own venal self-interest. She feels the anger rising, decides to harness it, to grab onto it and ride it hard for the finish.

"Fuck men! Fuck this baby! Fuck this world!"

She realizes she's screaming the words aloud when she sees Doctor Sanjay rear back like a horse spooked by a rattlesnake, his eyes unrecognizable, his face a frozen mask. But her unease is a luxury she can't afford as the next contraction batters her like a tsunami. His hands are on her shoulders, pressing her down onto the bed. But she wriggles out from under them and rolls onto her front. Any vestige of decorum banished by the intensity of the situation, she presses her face into the grimy pillow, pulls her knees up towards her chin and presents her rear end like a bitch in heat.

She'll never fully understand, or even properly remember, the rest of it. The pain, the exhaustion, the hormones, the emotion – all combining into a synapse-melting cocktail that permanently overpowers, and overwrites, her version of this experience in her hippocampus, amygdala and cerebellum. One minute she is an angry, scared woman, the next she's an exhausted, elated mother. She knows enough to know her world has changed forever, but her entire biological system is telling her not to worry, flushing her with celebratory endorphins.

She feels his hands gently helping her to roll over, easing her onto her back, lifting her head and sliding the pillow beneath it. When she opens her eyes, he is smiling once more, handing her a tiny little creature in what looks like a tea towel.

"It's a girl."

She weeps.

***

THE MAN

When he reaches the emergency exit, he finds another puddle of blood, and even some streaks on the door. He glances behind him, but the car park is deserted.

No going back. Come what may.

Pushing through the door he instinctively holds his breath, his pulse racing, but what greets him on the other side is not an end but instead a bizarre beginning. The staircase winds up and around ahead of him, but the handmade ramp that spans half its width is what catches his eye. Odds and sods of material, joined haphazardly to form a continuous smooth slope, it has a strangely unnerving effect on him. He recognizes something of himself, of his desperation, of his own fevered mind, in its construction. He tries not to look at it as he ascends, walking only on the steps and looking at the wall and the occasional windows - the paper, cardboard, or plastic bags taped over them preventing all but the rarest of glimpses of the world beyond the stairwell.

The climb goes on forever. He loses track of time. With no real daylight the penumbral gloom induces a trance-like state. It feels like the first time in forever that he hasn't been either in brutally bright sunshine or pitch-black darkness. He has the sensation of floating through water. He is underwater but not drowning - if anything he has already drowned. But this death holds no panic or fear, and is not the end. This walk is a procession to somewhere, something, else.

And then the labyrinth ends. A door, the final door, blocks his progress. No more stairs. No more ramp. He has the sensation of bobbing up for air, gasping and choking back the sting of saltwater as he tries to catch sight of land and a distant horizon. He steadies himself.

Just get to the hospital.

Well, he's done it. Suddenly that seems like the easy part. The uncertainty of what comes next, the unknown, flutters through his stomach. He steps forward, hand to the door handle.

The room beyond is empty save for two apparently occupied hospital beds and two attendant drips, the shapes on the beds mere indistinct lumps of clay in the half light. He limps closer. He's calling her name, but he's not sure if the words are even escaping his mouth or if they're trapped within, echoing in his skull. The first bed is a mess, wet with water and blood – but no Lucy. Instead a teenage boy, lying unconscious, possibly dead. A snarl from the other bed snaps his gaze from the pale, peaceful face of the unknown half-child.

Now he recognizes the room's other patient – Barry, his long frame stretched out on the bed. He watches impassively as his nemesis thrashes against his restraints, his hands and feet strapped tight to what appears to be a psychiatric ward bed, his blood flowing effortlessly from a bare arm into a collection bag beside the bed. The whole bed jumps, four locked wheels lifting off the linoleum in unison, as the captive patient throws his body against his bonds, back arching, head thrown back. The bed crashes back down, and Barry raises his head, catches sight of him properly for the first time. A wry smile at the irony of their role reversal flashes across his face and is gone.

"You."

"Where is she?"

"Get me out of this."

"Where's Lucy?"

"He's got her. That fucking psycho."

"Who?"

"That Doctor or whatever he is. Sanjay. He's a nut job."

"The baby – what about the baby?"

"I'll take you. Just get me out."

She always said he was too trusting. Right up to when she left and shacked up with Barry. He'd somehow worn that as a badge of honour in the months since. Refused to become the opposite, even as the world collapsed. Except for Tim. But he had trusted Tim. Too much even. In the end he'd only done what he had to, and only once Tim had proved himself to be too dangerous, too unstable, too untrustworthy. Then again, Barry had knocked him unconscious with a petrol can – not to mention stolen his wife.

"What are you waiting for?"

For you, Lucy.

He moves to the bed, refusing to meet Barry's eyes as he roughly pulls at the buckles holding him down.

"Take me."

When Barry sits up he can't read his eyes, but he forces himself to hold his gaze, not to flinch. He watches him pull the drip from his arm, the blood trickling back out of the tubing and spattering the floor. Barry stands and walks past him.

"Come on."

***

17th January 2021

I'm eating a Kit Kat. It's not my favourite chocolate bar but it's the only kind I have left. It's my special birthday treat. Assuming today is actually the 17th of January. That was always one thing we agreed on – that I was such a typical Capricorn. I never believed in horoscopes, certainly not the weekly star sign guides and advice columns in the papers and trashy magazines, but something about those pen portraits managed to so succinctly and accurately distil a complex personality into a few key facets. I'd read what it meant to be a Capricorn and it was like a mirror had been held up to my soul. Does it feel like that for everyone? Maybe. That's probably the skill of it.

It's cold up here on the roof, and the chocolate is rather cloying – in fact I've almost choked a couple of times. I think I'm a bit dehydrated, unfortunately I didn't bring any water with me and I emptied all the pans up here only yesterday – but the sunset is magnificent. A violently pink sky, tinged with deep orange and bright, almost white, yellow. Just enough clouds to provide some texture and context. Up here the world is practically silent. I feel entirely alone. But wonderfully so.

Happy birthday to me.

***

LUCY

As she holds the baby - *her* baby, her *daughter* - to her chest she imagines them a family: the two of them and the kind doctor who saved them both. She strokes the damp curls atop the child's head and looks up to see him watching intently.

She's about to ask after Barry, her hormones overriding her sense of unease and flooding her with gratitude for his help in carrying her here from the crash. But, before she can formulate the words, the door opens and there he is. His stance, the waves emanating from him, his piercing eyes, bring her back to herself. She clutches her baby tighter.

And then, from behind Barry's hulking frame, a ghost appears. He looks nothing like she remembers, in fact the intervening months have changed him almost beyond all recognition. Almost. He is changed, and yet he is still unmistakably him. Where Barry's eyes have become manic, his now resemble the glassy waters of a moonlit pool, secreted away in a woodland glade. Dark and serene, there is something ethereal, otherworldly about them. You could slip into them, naked and unnoticed, to bathe in the moonlight, but their depths would leave you altered.

A sob breaks free, and she catches it immediately, fearful one will lead to more, to an avalanche she won't be able to stop, that will bury them all.

All four of them stand and stare. No one moves, only their eyes - flitting from one to another. She sees the two new arrivals taking in the scene – her, the baby in her arms, the doctor by their side. It's her daughter who breaks the spell, a cough and then a healthy cry that pulls at her battered insides like a spring tide, the effect so visceral she gasps.

Before she can cry out Barry leaps forward and lands a swinging right hook that sends the doctor flying, knocking him sideways off his feet before he crumples to the ground. Frozen by shock, she's powerless to stop him as he scoops up her baby and bounds across the room, gorilla-like. A glance over his shoulder to check if he is pursued, and he is gone.

Ignoring her physical state, she rolls from the bed to her feet and staggers towards the door. Before she can reach it, her progress is halted, thin but deceptively strong arms encircling her, pinning her own to her sides and pulling her close in an unyielding but oddly gentle bearhug.

She allows him to guide her back to the bed. Suddenly she feels like a woman who has given birth, after hours of labour and a tortuous journey. She feels like she's been in a car crash. And then remembers she has. It already feels like a lifetime ago. She watches passively as he checks the doctor's breathing and then returns to her side.

"I'll get him back."

"She's a she. And she's yours."

He kisses her brow, and is gone.

***

THE MAN

Rage. Pure animal rage. He's not felt like this since, well, ever. Sure, there's some anger (at himself) and some shame mixed in there too – he can't quite believe he froze and let it all happen, let Barry take his daughter, but it was rather a lot to take in at the time, all told – but the emotion that powers his strides, fuels his hunt, is rage. Primal rage, the urge to defend his progeny at all costs. He can feel the pull of the DNA, felt it as soon as he saw the little bundle in her arms, something innate in those related double helixes that cannot, will not, be denied.

Just get her back.

The next room is empty. And the next after that. He's rushing, riding the adrenalin while he has it, terrified of letting Barry get too far. But he also knows he can't get ambushed, get caught off guard again. At each new door he takes a breath, listens, and then bursts through, jumping to one side and turning to face the other, in case his nemesis lies in wait. After three such entries to abandoned rooms, he gives up on the tactic. The rage is fading, and a creeping fear rises, beside a groundswell of held back exhaustion.

At the next door he turns the handle, pushes it open slowly at arm's length and takes a step back. Peering into the room from what he hopes is a safe distance he sees no movement, hears nothing. He can't see any doors out of this room, no exit for his quarry to have left by, but something draws him in. He steps across the threshold.

Like the others, this room is dim – an assortment of scraps covering the windows and blocking out the daylight. But something about the atmosphere is different, stands up the hairs on the back of his neck, a thick, cloying, closeness in the air that almost hums. While the surrounding rooms were practically completely empty, this one is filled with rows upon rows of beds. All are occupied. Men, women, children – of seemingly all ages and races – none of them moving. None of them breathing. None of them living.

The macabre menagerie leers at him, their faux-peacefulness inducing the exact opposite in him – unease bordering on outright terror.

They are patients. ***Were*** *patients.*

Now all corralled together, not in a morgue but in what he can only perceive to be a twisted familial tableau. The beds, the bodies (in what he can now see are various states of decay), seemingly grouped and posed as if conversing together, cloudy eyes open, arms spread wide or hands held out, heads tilted just so. No windows are open, but he could swear he feels a cold wind, or a rogue draft, snake around him, leaving a chilly imprint on his skin and triggering a shiver that's part cold, part exhaustion and part fear.

He realises he's been holding his breath. He inhales deeply, only to gag and choke on the stench and foul air. How had he not noticed that strangely familiar smell of death and decay?

A baby's cry breaks the spell, as it's wont to do. A cloud of flies takes to the air, a buzzing maelstrom of organized chaos.

She's close.

He's out of the room and sprinting towards the next door when he sees Barry step out into the corridor, the baby crying insistently in his arms. He skids painfully to a standstill, his ankle far from the only joint screaming its displeasure. He can only watch as Barry raises the bawling child high above his head. He's never known a feeling like it, hopes he never will again. Total and abject fear, a sickening helplessness that brings him to his knees, that makes him wish there was a god he believed in, to whom he could pray, who could somehow deliver his child from this. He feels in that moment like he himself is dying - a physical pain in his chest, the bottom dropping out of his stomach, an animal scream rising. But before it leaves his mouth, he sees Barry place the baby down gently on the floor, then turn and run, disappearing through the double doors at the far end of the corridor.

She smells like wet earth, her hair still curled in ringlets damp with fluid and blood, white streaks of wax-like vernix smeared across her back and limbs. He thought he'd be scared to hold her, to squeeze her too tight or hold her too loose, to drop her, to hurt her. He'd always been like that with other peoples' babies – nervous, aware of how precious they were to them even if not to him, not wanting to be the one that dropped them on their head. But now, his daughter in his arms, the doubt just melts away and he closes his eyes and breathes her in.

The truest moment of peace he has felt is not to last. The room of corpses intrudes, the images flashing through his consciousness, a strobing snuff film that brings him crashing back into a reality where Lucy has been left alone with a man who it seems has been living amongst the dead.

***

29th February 2021

I don't know if it's actually a leap year this year. Probably not. It's probably not even the 29th, or 28th, of February. It seemed somehow fitting though.

I need to write something now, and I'm not sure how it's going to go – so I'm just going to plough ahead and do it...

Okay. Fuck. Here goes...

When I'm not out hunting for supplies or busy fixing something here in the flat, when my focus slips and my mind starts to wander, normally when I'm warm and safe, that's when it intrudes. The spectre of the baby. Our baby. Your baby. I look back at the anguish you felt and all I can see is my own horrible, twisted reactions. The relief. The guilt at feeling relief. The self-loathing that came from that guilt. And now I can see, can see so clearly, that back then it was still all about me. I couldn't see beyond myself. I felt sad, sure. Sad for you. Sad for us. Slightly embarrassed and ashamed and disappointed. Worried about what to tell people, about what they'd say or think. But I didn't feel your pain. And I wasn't sad like you were. And through it all there was that part of me that felt relieved. That's what got me through it. But it's also what killed me inside. And I think it's also what killed us. It wasn't losing the baby that began the slow, painful decline of our relationship. It was my reaction to it. I see that now. And I'm sorry.

I'm so sorry, Lucy.

***

LUCY

When she wakes, she's not sure what it was that caused her to black out – exhaustion, blood loss or a total mental and emotional collapse caused by seeing her baby wrenched away from her. All she does know is her insides feel like a nest of baby vipers desperate to escape. She wants to vomit, to defecate, to run after her baby, and to sleep for a week. She turns her head and sees that the doctor, that Sanjay, is no longer lying crumpled on the floor.

"You're awake."

Thank God. It's him. He's alive, and he's still here with me.

"My baby?"

"I don't know I'm afraid. What happened? There's been no sign of anyone since I came to. Who was that man?"

She turns her head to the other side, towards his voice, and there he is, his slim form a horizontal line bisecting her vision as if he's a superhero flying across her eyeline. She ignores his question. His voice continues, and she finds she's grateful the silence is filled.

"Try not to worry."

She tries to sit up, and feels resistance.

His voice more insistent this time. "Take it easy, Lucy."

She gently flexes her limbs, anxious not to give much away, and finds that both wrists and both ankles are restrained. The vipers return.

"It's for your own well-being".

Fuck fuck fuck.

"Please. I just want to find my baby."

"It's OK. You need to rest. We'll just wait here. One of them will be back soon, I'm sure."

One of them? Which one? My ex-husband or my ex-lover?

She realizes all she really cares about is her baby. Whoever returns with her, or even if neither do, as long as the child is safe that is all that matters.

His back is to her, allowing her to work at the nylon straps holding her down as he prowls the far wall. As he passes the door, she sees he has pushed a chair against it, blocking the handle's movement. She pulls harder at her bonds. There is no give in them, no hint of a slipping, sliding clasp. He is opening drawers in the cabinets, the clink of glass and metal grating on her senses. A long, thin, glint of silver catches her eye then disappears into his pocket, his hand staying there, out of sight.

He walks back past the door, checking the chair still holds it closed with his free hand. Satisfied, he turns to face her at last.

"I'll be back shortly. Don't go anywhere!"

The last, a high-pitched chuckle at her expense, sends the snakes in her guts slithering in cold fury. Even more upsetting is the realization that, despite everything, she'd still rather not be left alone. She forces herself not to ask him to stay, and instead lies perfectly still, tracking his movements with her eyes as he crosses the room and leaves via the other, unbarricaded door through which the men from her past had burst in so unceremoniously moments earlier. How many moments, she realizes she has no idea.

She's barely begun to work at her restraints once more when she hears an anguished, drawn-out cry from beyond. She is transfixed by the keening wail, punctuated by spluttering, choking deep inhalations of breath summoned only to facilitate the next outpouring - the aural record of human grief since time immemorial. She recognizes in that sound the very emotions she felt when her newborn was snatched from her. Pain, loss, suffering, the sensation of the soul overpowering both body and mind in its writhing agony of impotence. In this moment she realizes she knows something of this man but that, conversely, she will never really know him.

Before she can return to the task at hand he is back, fresh smears of blood on his face, hands and clothes. He says nothing of the boy, of death, of failure. Instead, his face slowly relaxes, his breathing slowing and, when he has mastery of himself once more, he raises his head to look straight into her eyes.

"Don't worry. I won't let anything happen to you, Lucy."

***

THE DOCTOR

He feels like he's come back to himself, as if his very being, his consciousness, was a house, a home, that he had been away from for some time, perhaps on a long trip away, and that just now he has finally set foot back inside the threshold, put his bags down, stretched his back, taken a deep breath and finally said to himself, out loud even, "I'm home!"

The journey, this strange trip out of himself, sloughs off him, sluiced away like viscera on an operating table, to whirl down the drain and away, leaving everything clean and gleaming and renewed, if not new. The boy is dead. But he tried. Now he will just be one more companion, another reminder of his trip.

Who would have thought when he was admitted to the hospital he would end up be the lunatic running the asylum? His treatment had been effective; he could speak to the efficacy of those restraint straps for one thing. That had only been the beginning though. He'd taken the drugs, the injections, the counselling, the occasional cruelty and the even more occasional kindness - had balled it all up inside himself, like everything that had come in his life before. He'd studied the doctors, the nurses, even the patients, while there were still some alive. He'd always been a quick learner, if anything it had been the multi-dimensional power of his brain that had eventually led him here. Dropping out of medical school, drugs, gambling, bad decisions, worse friends, and yet through it all a thirst for knowledge. Eventually his scattergun approach to his own personal safety and welfare had caught up with him. A "catastrophic breakdown" they'd called it. A rebirth, as he now liked to think of it.

Eventually they'd stopped coming for him. He had just lain there, strapped in, the drugs wearing off, his throat dry, his stomach empty, the only sounds the creaks and bangs of the failing central systems of the hospital, echoing through the abandoned building. Before he'd become so weak he could never hope to free himself, he summoned enough energy to topple his own bed. Using his momentum to flip it sideways he made sure it collided with the wheeled table alongside, sending the tray of medical instruments tumbling to the ground. He too came crashing to the floor, unable to put his arms and hands out to break his fall he felt cheekbones, nose cartilage, and more, crunch. Like a dying snail he'd dragged himself across the floor, still strapped to the bed that now pinned him from above, his bloody trail glistening in the moonlight. A scalpel had saved him. A scalpel like the one in his hand right now.

"Don't worry. I won't let anything happen to you, Lucy."

He means it. He hopes she knows that, kids himself that he sees just the smallest hint of a smile form at the corners of her mouth. Despite the death of the kid, he still feels the remnants of the hormonal rush from the delivery. No one he had treated had ever survived. Until now. Not only had Lucy, his patient, survived – he had brought a new life into the world. He had delivered the baby. Delivered it unto her. It tapped into the part of him that fed his self-deification, that believed utterly in his own exceptionalism despite, and even because of, any evidence to the contrary.

The scalpel is light in his pocket. He wishes it was heavier, more suited to weighing down his hand, its innate gravity holding it out of sight. As it is, he must keep fighting the need to lift his hand.

Don't scare her. And don't show your cards too soon to whoever might try and come through that door.

Whoever it is, his plan is clear. He just hopes giving Lucy her baby back will outweigh killing whichever of the men is required to die. Then he can work on winning her over completely. Even he can concede there might yet be some work to do on that front.

She doesn't have all the pieces at her disposal, can't yet see the full picture. No bother. Soon enough.

The very thought of this ready-made family sets his brain whirring. He's lost track of when the last patient died, of how long he's been here alone. The radio calls had dried up months earlier, he'd almost given up on them after the traps he'd only narrowly escaped and the failures of all his treatments. But this was fate. That he'd charged the radio, that he had turned it on, that she had called, and he had answered – a voice from the ether. They had been set upon the same path, he can feel the convergence, their innate gravities pulling them ever closer.

With Lucy safely here with him, now he only has to wait to see who wins out and returns. Whoever it is will likely be weakened and, more importantly, unsuspecting. If they bring back the baby then Lucy will be happy, and – once he's done what has to be done - they can begin their new life as a family. After all, which single mother hasn't dreamed of a dashing doctor sweeping her off her feet? If the baby is gone, Lucy will be distraught. But that too plays into his hands. He will be the only shoulder left to cry on, the only one left who even knew her baby existed. He knows enough about grief and trauma to know the power of that bond.

Yes, perhaps that is the preferable option. Cleaner. Simpler. No child to complicate matters, to compete with for affection. Just the two of them. Rebuilding their lives out of the ashes.

Lucy hasn't said anything for a while. In fact, has she uttered a word since he came back? He looks to her, and sees her eyes are closed.

Yes, she's exhausted. She just needs to sleep. That'll make it easier, if she's not a witness, if he can make sure the story is just what it needs to be to set them off on the right path.

He forces himself to look away, he doesn't need to be staring at her while she sleeps. He needs to be on high alert, ready for action. He sidesteps to his left, putting the barricaded door in front of him and to his right, imagining a line of sight between the scalpel in his right pocket and the obstructed door handle.

One step, two steps, raise and stab. Aim for the carotid artery in his neck. Right side, most likely.

He imagines himself a knight, jousting. His horse black - galloping straight and true, foaming at the mouth - his lance raised and zeroing in on his opponent. No quarter asked, none given. To the death. To the victor... the spoils.

He shakes his head, not slowly in disappointment but vigorously, to wake himself up, to return to his senses. One thing he'd taken from his treatment – fight these pop culture daydreams. It was always in the middle of one when everything would unravel, when he'd find himself acting out the right fantasy in the wrong world.

Get a grip.

He hears something, footsteps from beyond the door. The handle moves, bangs against the chair, moves again, jerking harder and faster. It stops. A man's voice:

"What the fuck?"

If he had to guess he'd say not Barry.

Good.

Barry was the danger, really. The handle swings down again, and then jerks up and then immediately back down fast – enough to catch the chair in a fraction of movement, enough to squeeze home that advantage, the plastic back bending, the legs tilting and losing grip, and eventually the whole thing toppling to the floor only to be swept instantly aside as the door swings open.

***

THE MAN

He has never felt so self-conscious, desperate not to stumble, to trip, with his daughter cradled in his arms. He must make for a sight for sore eyes, limping down the corridor, as covered in bodily fluids as the new-born babe he carries. His emotions are fighting a running battle between the elation of fatherhood, and of safely recovering their child, and the gnawing, creeping dread of what he might find when he gets back to Lucy.

As he passes an open door the scene beyond trips the fear centre in his brain. Something about it, caught out of the corner of his eye, looks wrong. Feels wrong.

He takes a step backwards and peers into the room, subconsciously turning his upper body to shield the baby. There doesn't seem to be anyone in there, and now that he thinks about it he's pretty sure it wasn't movement that triggered his response, but something else. In spite of himself he steps into the room. It's darker than the corridor, and it takes a second for his eyes to pick out the shape that must have alerted his brain's temporal lobe. A hospital bed, upended on the floor, its jack-knifed humped back most likely the out of place angle that set his body's biological alarm bells ringing. Inside the room he scans from corner to corner - no Barry, no posed corpses, nothing out of place. Just the upside-down bed and, beside it, a toppled steel trolley table and scattered surgical implements. He's about to leave when he notices that pieces of material trail from the corners of the bed. On closer inspection they reveal themselves to be restraints – the tough nylon sliced clean through; the buckles still intact. The foot of the bed still holds a medical clipboard, an old style one, the digital tablets the staff had been so proud of when they visited early in Lucy's ill-fated pregnancy now obsolete since the virus caused the global loss of the internet, and even mains electricity...

The words upside down, he can't make out the typically scrawled handwriting of the medical professional even by craning his neck as far as he can without dropping his daughter. He squats and pulls the clipboard free.

Sanjay Veeraswamy

Paranoid schizophrenia, violent mania, psychosis

The patient's name and the diagnosis are all he needs to read before he's springing back to his feet and haring out of the door, the newborn bawling in the crook of his arm.

He's wheezing, his lungs burning, joints aching, his body finally forcing him to slow down after God only knows how many metres of gloomy corridors. As he eases to a brisk walk, a fast limp really, he recognizes the peeling, fading cardboard of a box that once held tinned tomatoes, its edges glowing, hinting at the bright sunshine that must be on the other side of the window.

The next corner leads back to the room. To her. To, he hopes, *them*. But also, perhaps, to *him*. He slows, then stops. He hikes the baby up onto his shoulder, gently stroking her back and shushing, calming her, quietening her down. When he's satisfied she's as quiet as he can hope for, he steps around the corner. Twenty metres in front of him is the door. He forces himself to walk slowly, as quietly as he can. Even so, every sound is amplified in the corridor like pennies tossed down a well.

He's at the door.

Here goes nothing...

The handle is jammed. It travels down an inch or so but no further, meeting unseen resistance on the other side. He yanks down harder, faster, the despair and frustration rising. He swears under his breath, can't help himself. He immediately regrets it. Not only for relinquishing what little uncertainty any foe beyond might feel, but even more for uttering a profanity within earshot of his only child, within minutes of her arrival into a world she needs to be protected from, and where instead she is being carried immediately into conflict.

He jerks the handle down hard, feels something beyond give just a fraction then slams the handle back down again. The double pump does the trick. The handle works free, and he stumbles into the room, his momentum propelling him unprepared through the doorway, his desire to keep hold of his baby, *their* baby, further impeding his balance.

As a result, he takes the scalpel not to the side of the neck as his attacker intends, but instead angled across the bony wing of his shoulder blade, where it slices skin, scrapes bone and then skids away, leaving a thin line of pared flesh that turns instantly from white to red.

As he turns, he expects to see anger, rabid and frothing, but instead he sees a cold zealousness in the look of his attacker. The scalpel is raised once more, and for a split second he imagines parrying the attack with the only object he has to hand – his daughter. He fights the automatic impulse to raise his hands, instead turning his back just in time, shielding the baby and taking the next stabbing blow fractionally to the side of his spine. Feeling the blade bury itself in the muscle he spins hard, and his assailant loses his grip.

Facing each other once more, he clutches his daughter to his chest and backs slowly away, his eyes never leaving Sanjay's snakelike gaze. Without breaking eye contact he shifts the child into the crook of his left arm, reaching behind with his right to grasp the scalpel, its handle protruding from his back and slick with blood. His fingers slipping, he pulls it out as straight as he can, feeling immediately faint as he does so. Sanjay's mask-like face gives almost nothing away, but the quickest of glances towards the door breaks the spell, betraying a nervousness that wasn't apparent before. He follows the imposter's gaze and lets out a choked yelp of relief when he sees Lucy lying on a hospital bed, eyes open and alert. Her voice, whispered as it is, is somehow so unexpected it feels like a shout in the silent room.

"Give her to me. Please."

"She's fine. He didn't hurt her."

"I just want to hold her."

He sidesteps to the bed, baby in one hand, scalpel in the other, eyes trained on the mental patient masquerading as a doctor. When he gets to Lucy's side, he realizes she's strapped down, held fast by familiar restraints, unable to reach for her child or even sit up. He walks backwards around the bed so that he can free her from the straps without turning his back to Sanjay. He hesitates, then gently places the tiny baby on Lucy's chest and grasps the first buckle. He sees Sanjay start to edge towards the door, but he doesn't stop pulling at the buckle. He just watches him. Watches him slowly sidle out through the doorway and disappear into the dingy corridor beyond. A second later the echoes without sing the ancient ballad of a man who has turned tail and run.

With the first restraint unbuckled Lucy's hand immediately shoots out, then slows to gently arrive on her baby's back. He's already working on the second strap when he hears the sobs begin. Big, ugly, messy sobs of love and relief. His fingers keep slipping on the buckle until he finally realizes they're wet with his own tears. He wipes his hand on his chest, and works the second restraint free.

***

12th April 2021

I was back up on the roof. It was hot. Really hot. And so very bright. I had been rationing my water and hadn't had a drop to drink in a couple of days. My head was pounding, I think a migraine was rearing its ugly head.

And then suddenly everything was in shadow. And I mean ***everything****. And when I looked up, I could see a black hole where the sun had been – and around it a glowing silver ring. It looked like a giant eye staring down at me, pinning me to the roof like a butterfly to a board.*

For a second, I thought I was dying, or the world was ending, or both. It didn't seem so bad, actually.

I must have passed out, as I woke up just as the sun was disappearing below the horizon. I felt sad, but I'm not sure if it was because the sun was setting or because it hadn't been destroyed for good.

***

PART THREE
DIVERGENCE

SANJAY

They ruined it. Ruined it all.

He was so close to having everything. His Lucy, his baby, his hospital. His future. Their future. Together. He imagines the scalpel finding its target, the blood spurting from that awful man's neck as he collapses at his feet. He leads Lucy by the hand, she's holding their child, they step over the body on their way out...

Then he remembers his other family. They have been with him through all of this. They never left him, never chose someone else, never betrayed him. He realizes he is almost at that very room, has been walking on autopilot back to the place where he feels safest, least alone. He quickens his pace, suddenly in a hurry for familiar faces, for their judgementless gazes.

But before he reaches the corner that will take him there, he smells something. A smell rare enough, yet somehow familiar and innate, that it stops him in his tracks. He sniffs the air.

Fire.

Despite being only metres from the macabre menagerie that has been his family for months, he chooses the only course of action he's never had to question – self-preservation.

The staircase is like a foreign land on his descent. The landscape has changed, not externally, but within him. Only hours ago, he was hauling the kid up here, with Lucy and Barry in tow. All was still possible. Now he has a cruel, childlike desire to slide down the ramp as fast as he can in the hope he'll black out and slam fatally into a wall at the bottom. He imagines the sensation of being out of control, of having made the decision to push off and now having so much momentum he can no longer stop, can't get off, can only ride it to its inevitable, inexorable conclusion. The relief of that decision having been made would be intoxicating. But he cannot make it. He's never been that brave.

***

THE MAN

He's not sure how long he's been asleep but for once, despite his total exhaustion, he's grateful to have woken up. His dreams had been plagued by spectres. He had been pursued by a one-legged man. He'd tried to flee but his leaden limbs would barely move, it was like he was wading through treacle. Unable to outrun his tormentor he'd turned to face him only to find himself confronted by Singh, his turban once more atop his head, a trickle of blood running from underneath it down past his ear. Hands raised; the figure had lurched towards him. He had reached out for the closest thing to hand, had held it out as an offering to placate his tormentor. It was a baby. His baby. When Singh took her, and turned away, he felt pure relief.

He wakes to a stomach-sickening panic. But Lucy is there, their daughter in her arms. The relief that wells up is soon submerged by a tide of guilt. He swallows it down.

Lucy hasn't noticed he's awake. She's just holding her daughter and staring at her. He watches them, not wanting to move or break the spell, the wholesome scene an antidote to the competing poisons eroding him from within.

He smells the fire before she does, takes a second to confirm he's not going mad or having a stroke. There's no mistaking it, the acrid taste at the back of his throat, his eyes beginning to itch, then sting, then water uncontrollably. The smoke tells a story - not a nostalgic woodsmoke-infused campfire tale of his youth but the bitter burn, the chemical suffused tang, of a 21st Century industrial accident.

He knows he ought to stand, to spring into action, but his body doesn't respond. He's so bone-crushingly tired. Nightmares or not, all he wants to do is sleep. He feels drugged, but he knows that's not the cause.

He closes his eyes, but not to sleep. Instead, he focuses in, times his breathing, mentally gathers himself back together. Eyes open, he is finally ready for what comes next.

"Lucy".

The word is little more than a croak. She doesn't notice, or at least doesn't acknowledge, her attention still locked onto the tiny wriggling, snuffling thing in her arms.

"Lucy. We have to go."

She turns and he can see her recoil ever so slightly, surprised that he is suddenly right by her side. Perhaps by more than that, he can't tell.

"Now."

***

4th January 2021

Some days I'm incredibly productive. I sneak out to hunt for supplies, or to tidy and organise the stash in the garage. Or I water, stake and prune the plants. Or I clean up the battery.

And other days I just sit in the flat in the dark and lose all track of time, only getting up to go to the loo or very occasionally to sip some rain-water or eat a small meal.

Today was the latter. It's night now, but it's been dark all day. At least in here. The sun was probably shining outside - I certainly didn't hear any rain - but I never saw it, thanks to the triple curtains I sewed together immediately after I made it clear I wasn't going to be part of the gang.

It should feel like a prison, and a self-imposed one at that, but in all honesty, it feels like a sanctuary. I'm not locking myself in, I'm locking them, it, everything, out. The only problem is the prison of the mind. There's no escaping that. I still have a tiny bit of alcohol of various shades left. After one of these days, I quite often resort to a bedtime drink or four.

Might as well call it bedtime now.

Cheers

***

LUCY

She closes her eyes, allows herself to imagine she's somewhere, anywhere, else. Just the gentle weight of her child in her arms, that strange yet familiar newborn smell. She had given up on this moment long ago. Then had barely dared to imagine it once more, even as her belly continued to swell until she thought she'd burst. She's grateful the room is quiet, enabling her daydream to continue a fraction longer: a clean bed, a bright airy room with a sea view from the huge bay windows. She'd always wanted to live by the sea. They'd even planned it when they thought they were going to be parents. Together. Then came Barry and the outbreak and everything else. She's glad the baby is not Barry's at least. The child feels entirely hers, but if this poor innocent must share her DNA with one of the men in her mother's life then...

She opens her eyes and there he is, standing stock still right next to them, staring at the baby. It takes her a second to get over the shock, as she surfaces from her fantasy life and back into the abandoned hospital, peopled with mad doctors and ex-lovers.

He's saying something about leaving, but she's too tired, too happy and too distracted, to listen, or to care.

'Now.'

Something about the way he says it cuts through, snapping her back to reality and triggering her innate sense of fear and base self-preservation - both now subtly changed, and multiplied a thousandfold, by her newfound maternal instinct. The jolt overcomes her exhaustion and inertia, sending a shockwave of adrenalin through her system.

He offers to take the baby, but she refuses, instead reluctantly accepting his support as she swings her legs over and slides off the bed, her child never leaving the crook of her arm. She can barely stand.

I feel as bad as he looks.

She laughs inwardly. It feels good.

As they walk together towards the door, she can't help but feel that something about him seems different. Not just his skeletal frame or his haggard appearance – although he certainly looks more like a vagrant, or some kind of mad false prophet, than the day she had left the flat – but something more subtle. If she is honest with herself, the truth is she had grown bored of him, bored of their life - or lack of it. Maybe she'd been depressed – with work, with losing a child. But now, now she hardly recognised this man – there was a wildness, a recklessness, a well of anger and sorrow, all swirling and eddying behind his eyes. And love. She could see it shining from him, energizing him. In the same way it was for her. Their child, this tiny baby in her arms, had already changed their lives forever.

***

THE MAN

The poisonous smell is soon joined by a haze that blurs their vision and stings their eyes. As they descend the stairs it slowly, insidiously solidifies into grey fingering tendrils and then billowing clouds of black. With every step the ambient temperature rises, the hot crackling intensifying. He's not sure if it's his imagination but he could swear the corrugated metal sections of the patchwork ramp are sweating, glowing, warping with the heat. He's too afraid to touch them, steering Lucy and the baby on to his right-hand side, against the wall and windows, placing himself between them and the ramp.

They're only halfway down and already the heat and smoke are becoming overpowering. He pulls the collar of his coat over his face with his free hand, the other guiding and supporting Lucy as she stumbles downwards, one step at a time, cradling their child in her arms, struggling to gently cover her tiny, wrinkled pink face with her sleeve without suffocating her.

Their descent becomes tortuously slow, and as they reach the next landing he knows they have a decision to make: turn around and retreat back up to the cooler, cleaner air above but risk being trapped; or push on through, harder and faster. It's no choice in the end. He's seen enough images of people trapped in buildings as they are consumed by fire or collapse into rubble. The silhouette of a man falling, falling, falling... it had burned itself onto his mind's eye then, and it resurfaces now.

"We need to go faster".

He expects resistance, is surprised when he sees no hint of pleading or fear - but instead an angry determination - take over not only her face but also suffuse the very set of her body. She doesn't question his decision, or even utter a word, she just hugs their child tighter, gently pushes his arm away and steps down onto the next step, and the next, and the next. She's almost running, her momentum close to overpowering her and sending her toppling forward down the staircase. He's about to call out to her when he realizes he's just watching, and instead he leaps down two steps at a time to catch up.

They reach the next landing together, and when he realizes she has no intention of stopping he too carries on, his longer stride and unencumbered state allowing him to overtake her and speed down towards the final door.

He can hardly see it, so thick and black is the smoke pouring through the gap between the door and its warping, sweating frame. He steps off the final step and onto the level floor of the corridor. His eyes are stinging and watering uncontrollably, his skin has stopped sweating and now feels like it is burning and blistering, his lungs and chest ache and his stomach is cramped tight like a spasming fist. He falls to his knees, crawling low where the air is infinitesimally clearer. He can hear his daughter crying from the stairs above.

Dragging himself on hands and knees he reaches the door, takes one slow breath - filtered as best he can through his coat – and leaps to his feet. In the same movement his hand, partially covered by the long sleeve of his coat, takes the handle and yanks it down. The burning pain is excruciating as he falls through the doorway.

Lying face down in a puddle of something – *water?* - he lifts his head to see the entire parking garage ablaze. Lines of spilt petrol burn in lightning bolt zig zags across the floor, a pile of broken wooden pallets, tyres and other detritus forms a giant bonfire against which has been pushed a handful of the smaller cars – the little hatchbacks and city run-arounds encircling the conflagration in supplication to the all-powerful element. Atop the pyre he can just about make out the blackened, warped shape of a jerry can, its spout pointing accusingly to the heavens, before it collapses in on itself like a black hole.

One of the cars explodes, sending a shower of sparks up like the Halloween fireworks displays that they used to watch burst into life across the bleak, black London cityscape from the balcony of their flat. He can see other clusters of cars, other fires, dotted all around the garage. The acoustics magnify the roar and crackle, the space a skull afflicted by a violent tinnitus. The wind from without is feeding and fanning the flames, the draft rushing in down the ramp that forms the open entrance to the garage and breathing life into the fires.

He hears the cries of his child again, and rolls over to see Lucy standing over him. She screams. Her terror is so genuine – and her gaze so fixed directly on him - that he checks himself instinctively, his hands to his face, his eyes scanning his body. His clothes are dark and wet, but when he brings his hands back from his face he realizes they are a dark, dirty red. As he gets to his feet, she backs away from him.

"It's OK. I'm OK."

He touches his face again, looks down at the puddle.

"It's not mine."

He sees her shrink. The sudden relaxation turning dangerous, transforming into a slump he's only just in time to save her from. He sits her down, but she refuses to let him relieve her of the burden in her arms.

"Just a minute."

"Thirty seconds, Lucy. Then we run."

"Okay."

"I mean it. We run. Seriously fucking fast. And we don't stop until we are out. All three of us. Okay?"

"Yes. Run." She looks at him. "Fucking fast."

The hint of a smile.

***

THE MAN

The purity of the goal, its singular simplicity, makes everything else – the heat and roar of the fires, the smell of the swirling, blinding, black smoke – melt away. It's just the three of them, running for the light. Cars may have exploded with the heat and the flames, others may have spontaneously erupted into cacophonous sons et lumières as their alarms went off and windows shattered, he'll never remember or know for sure. They ran, Lucy somehow keeping pace as if she'd spent the last nine months training for a marathon rather than preparing to bring a child into the world. At one point he fancied he saw someone, something, dancing through the smoke and fire, like a shadow cast on an ancient cave wall.

Whatever the truth of it, for all that truth might be worth, they made it to the exit ramp. One last sprint up the cement slope and they are vomited out into the impossibly fresh, clear air of another perfectly bright day.

He can tell she is spent, and he would dearly love to just let her rest, breathe, recover. But he's desperate to put more distance between them and the building. She finally allows him to take their baby and then he offers her his back, bending at the knees, and she understands. With one arm bent back to support her rump and the other holding their baby girl he staggers around the corner away from the where the mouth of the car park whistles and roars as the oxygen rushes in to fan the flames, their orange glow flickering behind the peeling makeshift blinds of the lower storey windows like candlelight in a pumpkin.

He crosses the road to the far pavement, keen not only to get as far away from the hospital as possible but also to give a wide berth to the corpses and carnage of the ambulance crash scene. He leads her up over the pavement and the grass verge, feeling her grip tighten around his neck as they pass parallel to the vehicle, its roof lights visible but the line of sight to the attendant dead bodies thankfully blocked by the long-abandoned cars that crowd the edge of the road, discarded in a hurry many months ago, no rhyme nor reason to their contrasting angles.

When they've gone far enough, when he can feel her grasp loosen and his knees start to wobble, he stops and lets her down. Only then does he realise the baby is asleep. Gently, silently, with the joyful fear of a new parent, he shows her the bundle – and they share a smile that collapses into an exhausted, overwrought combination of laughter and tears they fight to control for fear of waking the child.

They sit down on the kerb, and he hands her back their daughter, and they just sit there and look at her together. He's still staring at this impossible little thing when Lucy's fingers pinch his wrist. Instinctively he looks up.

"He's there!"

But he can't see anyone.

"There, in the window!"

His eyes skip across the hospital façade, not tracking logically, line by line, but in random zig zags, only partially focussed, receptive to movement or change. Nothing.

"He's gone."

He's still looking, but she takes his silence for doubt.

"I'm not mad. He was there. Doct... Sanjay. Him."

"He's not there now."

"He was. Too high."

"Let's go."

***

27th November 2020

I may still have some alcohol left but one thing I really miss is coffee. The last jar of instant ran out ages ago, and I've not found any more on my travels - but those ersatz granules don't even really count. No, I mean proper freshly ground roast beans, that dark, bittersweet hit of real espresso.

Do you remember the withdrawal symptoms we got early on in aftermath of The Event, after we first ran out and it was too dangerous to venture out? The headaches that slowly crept up on us in the mornings, the dizziness and irregular heartbeats... it took us a while to work out what it was, that it wasn't a panic attack or some kind of physical manifestation of the mental and emotional stress of the collapse of the world. That first week was the worst, but I'm still not sure I've ever fully recovered. I miss it. I crave it. I tried acorn coffee for a bit - they're plentiful around here it least. Not only was it a huge effort to prepare, it tasted pretty terrible, and it's not even caffeinated. I guess I could try growing some kind of substitute, say chicory, but what's the point, it's still not caffeinated. Once I risked hiking all the way down the hill and sneaked into the cafes, supermarkets and mini markets just on the hunt for beans. It took me all night, and I found none at all.

The only other solution I can think of is to try and source a coffee or tea plant. Do we even have those in this country? They probably would never have grown here, but these days the weather is so different they might just flourish. I wonder if the big garden centre way out of town might have stocked them? If it did, I bet there are still some left.

That's what I'll do. I need a project anyway. It'll take me a couple of days to walk there and back safely. I'll pack up some supplies and camp en route.

Wish me luck...

***

SANJAY

He's not sure what made him return. He was halfway down the stairs and coping with the heat and smoke when he decided to go back. Perhaps it was the pull of family, after all. Not Lucy and the baby, but those he had cared for and kept 'alive' even after their inevitable deaths. His patients. His family. In truth, the only real family he'd ever had. They'd kept him company, kept him sane. At the very least he should say goodbye. He wouldn't just disappear and leave them, not like his own parents had.

And so, it is from *their* room – his one true family - that he watches his fantasy family exit the hospital, Lucy and the baby hoisted high on *his* back like villagers escaping a flood. He doesn't wave goodbye, just watches them until he fancies she might have seen him and then retreats back from the single exposed pane of glass, moving back once more from light into shadow.

He takes his time making his final rounds, straightening the cuffs and collars, hems and necklines of the men, women and children he has collected around him. He says his goodbyes to each and every one of them, thanking them by name for entrusting themselves to his care and apologizing for not being able to do more for them, then or now. However, he does not covet the role of the brave captain on deck, going down with the sinking ship.

By now the staircase will be impassable. But he hasn't lived in this hospital for months without preparing an escape route. It takes him several minutes to navigate the endless maze of corridors but eventually he reaches a staircase far on the other side of the building. Instead of descending he heads up, for here there are two further flights of stairs, two more floors, which exist nowhere else in the hospital. They are less decorated, more industrial, and at the top a heavy metal door leads out onto the rooftop. He pauses in the middle of the expanse, the giant white painted 'H' unnoticed beneath his feet as he stands and slowly turns to take one last look at the breath-taking panoramic view of London from this vantage point. His rotation complete, he crosses the helipad to the cast iron fire escape stairs at the far corner and starts down them without a backwards glance.

***

LUCY

She has no idea where they're going, but she's happy just to try and plant one foot in front of another and slowly but surely put some distance between them and the hospital. Anything is better than being in that place. She's still coughing from the effects of the smoke, even though the air is now mercifully clean. Thankfully her daughter, the tiny little thing - back in her arms where she belongs, and from whence she'll never go again - is sleeping soundly with no sign of a wheeze. He'd offered to carry one, or both, of them again - but she was having none of it.

After what seemed like weeks, but must have been less than fourty-eight hours, in that artificially dingy building she should be grateful to feel the warm sun on her skin. But as it rises higher into the sky, and the last lingering wisps of cloud burn off, the heat quickly becomes oppressive. Her skin, where it's kissed by the direct rays of the sun, reliving the pain of their escape from the fire.

She sees the three of them as an observer, not so much an out of body experience as a change of camera angle from a first to third person point of view, and it makes her want to laugh. Soot smudged, bruised and bloodied; they limp away from the twisted mausoleum masquerading as a hospital. She remembers how she imagined this moment might be when they first found out she was pregnant, that fateful first time around,, when they were still together, when the world still made some kind of sense – or at least when they thought it did, didn't know any better. Well, the scales had certainly fallen from her eyes now. And something about the focus in his gaze suggested she wasn't the only one who had been transformed by all this. She'd never picked him for a potential diamond, someone who would harden, gain rare clarity, under pressure. But he exuded a purposefulness, a singlemindedness, that she'd never seen in him when their lives had revolved around what holidays to plan or what take away to order. She's pleased. Not just for him, although she is glad that he's found a way to navigate this new universe, but selfishly for her and her child. She'd thought he was too weak, too woolly, and she'd come to realise that would be a death sentence for the child forming in her womb. Now she can see that their daughter might just have a chance, if she gets the best of the pair of them.

Heaven help her if she gets the worst.

Her daughter, *their* daughter, wakes and immediately starts crying – and she realizes they are at the gate to the park.

***

THE MAN

He can't help but notice the strange expression on Lucy's face as they drag themselves up the road, away from that awful hospital. He gave up trying to read her a long time ago, no point getting back into all that now. He's got this far by breaking everything down into simple, achievable single objectives. He made it to the hospital. He found Lucy. He got her and the baby out of there. Now he has to get them safe.

That's it. Get them safe. Nothing else matters.

Everything else is a distraction. And being distracted is a shortcut to death, the evidence of that written in blood everywhere you choose to look.

Like a blinkered carthorse, the brewer's dray that still occasionally trod the streets where he grew up, he must just stay the path and remain calm. He's learnt that by now - that survival involves cutting out the extraneous, filtering out the white noise and the background chatter, the doubt, the other paths, and focusing in on the only things that matter.

He stops just within the confines of the park and looks back. Lucy is standing on the threshold, and as the baby wakes and starts to cry he feels the sudden terror that he has doomed them all by turning around – he Orpheus, she Eurydice, that expensive classical education now contributing nothing but nightmares. But no, she takes a step into the park, and then another. And, before he knows it, she is past him and he has to jog to catch them up.

"Are we actually going somewhere?"

"Yes. Sorry. Follow me."

"I always hated it when you did that, you know?"

"Sorry. Did what?"

"That! Said sorry. For everything."

"Oh. I see. Yes. I'm..."

He almost does it again, but catches the word in time. It's been so long since he's really spoken to anyone properly, let alone her, his voice seems foreign to him - like the man he saw in the mirror.

But when she frowns at him in that gently accusing, almost mocking, way of hers he feels himself again, knows his place in the universe once more. At least in that moment, anyway.

"Let's rest for a bit. Here, sit down."

They're in a shady copse, one of the once-tended clusters of trees and bushes that has been allowed to intertwine, dancing together towards the sun in a tangled embrace of branches and leaves, as humanity's husbandry faded away. He gestures her to a log, and she doesn't resist. In fact, rather than sit perched on it, she eases herself down onto the ground on her elbows, still never relinquishing her hold on their baby, and lies down, the log supporting her head and neck. She looks dog-tired, and he sees her eyes slowly close as she hugs the child to her bosom.

"I'm not going far, but I think you could do with some water. And I'll see if I can find something to eat. There should at least be some berries around here somewhere."

She murmurs what sounds like assent.

The first few places he checks yield nothing. Any organic receptacle, be it a giant lily pad or the nook of a tree, has seemingly been incapable of retaining any semblance of clean rainwater since the last storm. Then he remembers the playground. He passed it on his way from the secret garden to the hospital, and made a mental note of what looked like pots, pans and even a big red plastic bucket perched atop the squat little maintenance hut beside the sandpit. He'd surmised they'd been placed there some time earlier, perhaps by the same person who'd tended the garden. Something about the way they were arrayed burrowed into his brain like a tick, unnoticed and malignant.

The wildness of the park is disorientating. In a bid not to get lost he attempts to take his bearings using the sun, and the shadows it casts from the tallest and straightest trees. Lucy and the baby are almost directly behind him, at least he thinks so, as he lines himself up with where he estimates the playground lies. Suddenly conscious he's been zig zagging and hopping between less and less likely water sources without paying due attention to where he's going, he resolves not to deviate from this path. He'll march straight forward until he either hits the playground or he doesn't. And then he'll turn one hundred and eighty degrees and retrace his steps. He commits the clearing in which he now stands to memory – finding troll-like faces in the gnarled bark of the trees and conjuring up a spooky fairy tale tableau in their alignment that he hopes he'll recognise again.

Not for the first time, he concentrates on putting one foot in front of another, his entire journey *to* here, and *from* there, made up of just one stride at a time. He banishes Lucy and the baby to the back of his mind. Actively worrying about them now will only distract him. They can be his motivation without interfering with his present focus.

Get to the playground. Find the water.

He passes a bandstand. It looks like the same one as on his last trip through the park, but he can't be sure. It doesn't feel possible to be sure about anything in here. He wishes he had a ball of yarn with him, a cord he could have tied to the tree where Lucy and his daughter are resting. Wishes he could play it out behind him and feel the reassuring thread running between his fingers, anchoring him, tethering him to the reality retreating further behind him with every step.

Then, just as he's resolving to perform his about-face, he steps through a screen of tall bushes and there, opening out before him like the buffalo-dotted prairies of the Wild West, is the playground. The sad little congregation of faded metal frames should be depressing to behold. No children have played here for months, in all likelihood they never will again. And yet the sight gives him renewed hope. He found it. For the first time in his life, he feels the triumphant elation of a father who has succeeded in providing for his family, the primal hunter-gatherer feedback loop that tells him this is what your role is now, and it is its own reward.

Feeling ten foot tall he strides purposefully through the gap in the waist-high metal fence where once a gate kept toddlers imprisoned. Between the seesaw and the slide, the swing set a deserted gallows away to his right, he draws ever closer to the hut. The hut where the pots and pans stand sentry duty.

The bucket. Where's the bucket?

"I wondered if I'd ever see you again."

Barry's appearance on that low flat roof provokes actual physical pain, a sharp jolt lancing down from inside his skull, just above his left eye, and travelling down through his body to pin his foot to the ground. Had he been alone he might have spent several minutes fixating on whether he was having a stroke, an aneurism, the start of a migraine or had finally succumbed to a new form of self-fulfilling hypochondria (*perhaps Munchausen's?*). Instead, he wills the pain back up into his brain and seals it off and, his body distracted by the sudden vertigo induced by this effort, he forces himself to pull his foot up and take a step forward.

He looks up just in time to see Barry leap from the roof and land in the sandpit, the impact setting off a flurry of miniature sandstorms around his feet. Arms wide, knees bent, he shuffles forward in a wrestler's pose, his eyes never breaking gaze.

He's never strictly been a coward, as such. But he has always been careful to weigh up pros and cons and likely outcomes, and to occasionally pick the path of least resistance. Lucy would attest to that, it was one of the things that drove her mad about him. But Lucy, that self same Lucy who left him for this scout leader on steroids, needs water.

There's water here. On that roof. And Barry isn't just going to let me run away. Not this time.

He takes a single step forward and lets out a low grunt as his brain and voice finally catch up to the decision his body has already made.

So, this is it then.

They circle each other, the only audience for their pathetic gladiatorial contest the disused playground equipment and a flock of parakeets that skims low over their heads and disappears into the branches of a fruiting tree, their squawking calls echoing off the cement and tarmac before being swallowed by the surrounding belt of dense foliage.

He can feel the adrenalin spiking, his body channelling all his testosterone, his biology doing its best to boost his chances of survival. He fights the urge to rush in, to attack with no plan for victory. He also resists calling out – he'd love to find the right words to challenge, to mock, to impress, to give himself courage, but he knows he won't. This isn't about style, or panache, or one-upmanship, or anything other than finding a way, any way, no matter how dark or dirty, to win out. He needs to win. For perhaps the first time in his life he really needs to win. Because losing means the end.

He realises he's not just terrified by that realization, he's energised by it, empowered by it.

Fuck it. I have to kill Barry.

Now that he knows the truth of it, his mind clears. He sees the man in front of him and feels not the jealous hatred of a love rival, nor the fear of one who has been bullied, but instead the cold, calm dispassionate certainty that he is the hunter and this man has become his prey. That he will live, and Barry will die. And the last, so deeply buried that he doesn't even know it is there - that there is no other option, because he is a father now and he will kill for that.

Barry's right hand swings faster than it has any right to, the fist snapping his head back when it connects with his left cheek. The next, a tight left, catches him on the solar plexus and takes the wind from him, doubling him over. Something hard and bony (*a knee?*) catches him a glancing blow, mercifully ricocheting off the corner of his skull rather than catching him flush in the face and shattering his nose as no doubt intended.

He's able to stagger away, knows that if that last strike had been clean that would have been game over. Maybe three seconds, tops. That's all it would have taken, and he'd have been down and out.

But Barry is dancing on the spot, smiling, taking his time.

He thinks he's fucking Muhammad Ali.

He runs, darting left and behind the chalet-style base of the 'big slide' and out of sight. He can hear Barry following.

Good.

He dances between the wide metal legs of the frame of the swings, limboing beneath the metal crossbeam, and as Barry ducks down and tries to follow him he launches the heavy rubber seat of the swing hard into his face. He can hear the crunch as Barry's nose breaks, an immediate spray of blood followed, a split second later, by a cascade of the stuff.

Barry's roar is one of wounded pride more than mortal injury, but it affords an opening – and he doesn't pass up the opportunity. He wraps the chains of the swing around his enemy's neck, twisting and tightening, watching the links start to press into the flesh. The understanding that he is about to take a life, deliberately – not like the fated swing of the spanner that did for Singh – causes an infinitesimally small reversal in his grip, in the pressure on Barry's neck. He senses his mistake, his subconscious weakness, and redoubles his efforts just as Barry's hands shoot out, giving up trying to remove the chain and instead searching for his attacker's eyes. Ragged nails scratch at his face as he turns his head desperately to keep the fingers from homing in on their target. Barry has his skull in his grip now, his fingers stretching like the tentacles of an octopus.

He lets go of the chain and punches Barry as hard as he can in the face, right on his majestically broken nose. He feels the blood whip from his knuckles on the follow through, spattering the ground. Barry relinquishes his grip on his skull. He gets one more quick jab in, catching him on the corner of his eye, and turns and runs once more.

He fights to stay in his body, can feel himself drifting up and away to observe from way up in the clouds. He can see how ludicrous it all looks from up there, as they chase each other through the playground. But he can also see his death. He can't be up there. He needs to be down here. In the dirt. Fighting for his life.

Barry catches up to him at the seesaw. They resume their simian posturing, feinting one way then the other in half-crouches that make his thighs burn. The blood flow has slowed from Barry's nose, and he can see the confidence returning to his foe – they both know the longer this contest goes on the worse his chances of victory.

Barry takes a step forward. And that's when he sees it. His chance. He slams both his palms down on the seat of the seesaw in front of him – sending the far end flying up and catching Barry under the jaw, snapping it shut, his teeth shearing off a corner of his lolling tongue. As Barry turns away and drops to his haunches, hands to his face, he grabs the end of the seesaw and hauls it up from below his knees to way above his head. The far end swings down in a fast, vicious arc right on the crown of Barry's head. He doesn't stop there. He pumps his arms maniacally up and down, to the full extent of their reach, until they will no longer obey, the lactic acid flooding his muscles and telling him to stop, you can stop, he's already dead. Barry's head is a bloodied mess where the metal and plastic has battered it out of shape, cracking it like an egg.

His manic euphoria drains away. But as he waits for it to be replaced with a sickening dread and mounting shame he finds that nothing comes. Nothing - he feels nothing, not even numb. He's not deep in shock, he just feels the pure calm of an absence of any base emotion. This realization, when it comes, breaks the spell. He doesn't feel sick, if anything he feels a kernel of triumphant joy – and that he fights back down. He's not yet prepared to celebrate taking another life. Even Barry's. But he can sense his body coursing with energy at having prevailed – and protected his progeny. He channels this unexpected boon, hauling himself up onto the flat roof of the maintenance shed, before his body finally crashes hard and he lies down in the sun to sleep.

***

THE MAN

The pots and pans are mostly full. Only the bucket, tipped on its side, is empty. Barry must have drunk it dry before he got there. Or maybe it got knocked over when he jumped down from the roof. Either way, it's the biggest receptacle so he decants the contents of all the other vessels into it before realising he's stuck up on the roof with a full bucket and no easy way down. In the end he balances the pail right on the edge of the roof, tosses the biggest of the empty saucepans into the sand and lowers himself down. Using the pan as a step he's just able to reach up on tiptoes and slide the bucket off the edge of the roof and onto his tented fingertips. Once it's safely in his hands he rewards himself with a small sip.

He carries the bucket back by its worn-out little handle – the palm of his spare hand pressed flat underneath supports it and take the weight off, ready to keep it balanced and preserve the contents should it break off or fail. He spies some brambles sporting a few passable blackberries – and pauses to gather enough to fill his pockets. As he sets off once more, he remembers reading that scientists had found that people lost in the wilderness had an innate tendency to walk in circles. He makes a conscious effort to look up, check the sun, scan for reference points and fix his eyes on a point to aim for that he feels confident is on the path back.

Whatever you do, don't get lost.

He enters a clearing and – although the light seems different, the air more of a murky, damp blur - his imagination is able to bring to life the troll-like faces in the trees once again. He is indeed on track, his straight line has miraculously held true. From there it doesn't take him long to retrace the final few hundred metres back to his family.

He returns to find Lucy asleep, the baby at her breast likewise, her mother's milk drying at the corner of her mouth. He carefully puts the bucket down in the shade of the log, close at hand but not so close that she might knock it over if she wakes suddenly. He finds a large flat leaf, places it next to the bucket and piles the blackberries on top.

He should be standing guard but, instead of studying the undergrowth surrounding them for any glimpses of movement or listening intently for a snapped twig or rustling leaves, he can only stand and stare at the woman and baby asleep against the tree trunk and listen to the syncopated murmur of their breathing.

***

THE MAN

He wakes to discover he's done something he's never done before – slept standing up. He'd always assumed it was some kind of urban legend, a convenient metaphor rather than a reality. He's not sure if it's the stance he was in, or the roll call of injuries he's sustained over the last few days, but his entire body is crying out in pain. He has to force himself not to move too suddenly, but instead to gently flex each muscle and roll each joint, like an android coming to life and exploring each part of its exoskeleton in perfect isolation. He'd woken up stiff and sore enough times in the past and not taken heed – and had almost always paid the price, his neck or back the main culprits, the most likely to completely seize up and leave him partially incapacitated for days.

Can't afford that now.

At least when he has worked his neck loose enough to risk turning his head, he is able to see that Lucy and their daughter are still there. Safe. Asleep. Lucy sporting a matching pair of purple smears at each corner of her mouth, the pile of blackberries depleted beside her. He stands and watches them as he slowly works his way down his body, stretching out all the kinks as best he can.

He's not quite finished, still too nervous to make any extended or sudden movements, when they stir - and first one then the other wakes.

'How are you feeling?"

She smiles, rearranging the baby in her arms. It resumes its noisy suckling.

"Tired. Thanks for the berries. And the water."

"We should go soon. I'm not sure how safe it is here."

As he's speaking, he watches her eyes as they dwell on first his face and then take in his stance. Something causes her to cock her head, squint and frown. He can see a question bubbling to the surface...

"What is it?"

"What?"

"You. You seem... different. What happened?"

"I'm sorry I was gone so long. It was harder to find water than I thought."

"Don't do that."

"What"

"Dodge the question. You always used to. And I always hated it. I think we're a bit fucking beyond that by now, don't you?"

"Lucy!"

His raised eyebrows further exaggerate his stage-look to the baby.

"Sorry. But she doesn't care."

"No, she's happy as Larry."

As soon as the phrase is out of his mouth, he wishes he could recall it. He can feel the similarity, the assonance of that name dredging up the conflicting emotions of the violence of which he's just been a very active part. He fights to keep his face devoid of expression, settling on what he hopes is a wry smile but suspects just looks creepy and fake.

"So, are you going to tell me or not?"

"Tell you?"

"What happened while you were gone. While we were asleep."

"Later. We need to go first. I'll tell you later. When we're somewhere safer."

"Ha! Like where?"

"Actually, I do have an idea."

"We're not going back to the flat to play happy families with you, if that's what you think!"

"No. Somewhere else. We... we can't go back there."

He sees the plants arcing from his balcony, the sound of the pots smashing on the road below painfully loud in his memory. He doesn't want to cry. Not here and now, over this. Not like this. He turns away to hide the shame of his sadness.

She'll never know how grateful he is that she doesn't ask any more.

***

5th January 2021

I think you saved us by leaving. Not us as a couple, obviously. That ship had already sailed, I fear. But us as individuals. And not just metaphorically. I really think I've only survived because I've been able to focus only on myself. I hope you too have made it this far - with or without (OK, preferably without) Barry - that I'm writing to that tough, smart Lucy that always seemed to make the right decisions, Lucy the survivor, and not a ghost, a corpse, yet another casualty of the end of the world as we know it. I'm sure you have. If I've learned to survive then surely you have.

But can you imagine trying to survive together in this tiny flat, trapped on the top floor and surrounded by the capricious cruelty and violence of our former neighbours?

There's no room for compromise in this new world. No time for doubt or indecision. I move silently in the dark of the night. I sit silently with the curtains closed. I eat and drink the bare minimum to make my supplies last as long as possible. Everything I do to survive is only possible because I do it alone. Undistracted by worrying for another. Protected from the paralysing fear of indecision. Able to shape my own reality and my own morality, free from the conscience that comes with responsibility to another.

I live in monastic silence, except for the odd conversation with Mr Tibbles or myself. This diary provides a more regular outlet for my words and a chance to communicate with you. If you had stayed the arguments would only have got worse. We'd have never been able to remain undetected. And we'd have been forced into a choice - stay and fight (surely suicide), run (to where? for how long?) or join one of the gangs, something I know neither of us could have stomached.

Lone wolf or pack animal are the only choices. Mating pairs are easy prey.

***

LUCY

She's angry. Angry that she's worried about him. She's not felt that for a long time. Doesn't want to feel it now. She's just given birth. She has a tiny baby girl depending on her for every aspect of her frail existence, for her very survival. And yet she's worried about *him*. And from all he's said, or not said, she knows she's right to. Something bad has happened. Several things if she had to guess. Something just now, while he was foraging. And something longer ago, back at the flat, after she had left.

Something has broken in him. Should I be scared of this man?

He's pacing impatiently at the edge of the clearing, the red plastic bucket banging awkwardly against his knee, but she's determined not to rush on his account. Her stomach feels crampy, the blackberries and rainwater sloshing around uncomfortably and ,if anything, increasing her hunger and discomfort. She starts to manoeuvre herself up, the baby still in the crook of her arm, when he realises she needs help. He darts back over, suddenly full of nervous energy, reminding her rather too much of Barry. She lets him offer his free arm, hauls herself upright with his help, but then gently nudges him away. She's grateful he takes the hint and retreats back to the treeline. She straightens up, steeling herself for more walking. When the baby – *she really needs a name* – starts mewling she holds her gently to her chest and shushes in her ear, taking this as her cue to start walking, to get them safely away from this place that feels as if it's got darker and colder.

He parts the first few branches for her, and she steps from the glade into the darkness of the undergrowth that's kept them invisible for the last few hours. She follows his jinking path between trees and bushes, somewhere between a trance and autopilot – his occasional barked warnings about tree roots or other trip hazards the only thing keeping her tethered to reality. She forces herself to keep her eyes trained on the small of his back, as if they are roped together like a pair of mountaineers or potholers.

When they emerge into the bright sunlight of the open grass, she realises she has no idea how long it took to make their way through the trees. It feels like it went on forever, that dazed tramp through the penumbra, her feet thankful for the springy loam beneath them, the cool of the gloom by turns pleasant and chilling. The sun is painfully bright, but the warmth is welcome. A cry from her arms and she notices the sun is directly in the eyes of the babe at her breast. She turns her back to the sun to shade the child and sidesteps to where he is standing and staring into the middle distance.

"There."

She can't see anything, her eyes still struggling with the glare. And then...

...there it is, nestled in the distant dark green wall of foliage that cuts across the horizon in front of them. The glint of metal, dull black with specks of brightly shining silver where the finish has worn off and, most invitingly of all, the faded gold letters.

"The community garden?"

"Yup."

He seems calmer. Less like Barry and more like how she remembers him, how he was before everything. Maybe it's just the late afternoon sun, dropping low and bathing everything in a golden wash, but he definitely seems gentler somehow. Warmer. Happier. Even if she wasn't so exhausted, she feels like she'd blindly follow this iteration of him. She'd trust him on this.

Funny how we all act like each person is just a single entity.

She's not sure where the thought came from, nor whether it's the ravings of an exhausted new mum or a rare moment of transcendent clarity. He puts his arm around her shoulders and this time she doesn't resist. She leans into him, allowing him to take a tiny bit of her weight and to control her balance and momentum as they step forward in unison. The sun dips behind the treeline ahead and the baby falls silent. They reach the gate as the shadows all around them fade, bleeding into one another, unnoticed by the trio, until they blend into a single expanse of semi-dark as the sun sets and the night steals over the land.

***

THE MAN

He wants to just sink to the turf and cry, or sleep, or both. But this is no time to indulge in personal histrionics. Lucy and the baby need him. She's still dehydrated, and completely exhausted. Thankfully their tiny little girl seems in rude health despite everything, a minor miracle that she latched on and suckled as if born to it. But if that's to continue then he needs to look after Lucy.

He ushers them to a corner of the garden, where the grass is soft and springy and still pleasantly warm from the recently departed sun. There he sits Lucy down and makes her drink several careful, slow sips of water from the bucket and eat the remaining handful of blackberries from his pocket that have just about survived the walk. This done, he eases her down so she can lie on the grass with the baby on her chest. He has aligned her with the slope so that her head is marginally above her feet – but even so it looks awkward. He heads into the greenhouse and re-emerges with a big plastic sack of topsoil that he manoeuvres under her head as a makeshift pillow. Her eyes seem grateful. She's asleep in seconds.

As she and the baby sleep – he remembers being told by everyone they knew, way back when they first thought they were going to be parents, when they jinxed it by letting people know way too early, that you should always sleep when the baby sleeps – he takes a tour of his miniature Eden. He wants to take stock of what he has, what they can use, eat, grow, survive on. The audit is intended to make him feel better, to give him confidence in his decision to bring them here. But as he wanders, staggers really (for he certainly isn't able to affect a stroll), he can sense a rising tide of dread lapping at the shore of his subconscious, sucking at the pebbles and drawing them into the deep. Each wave rising higher than the last, darkening the beach. And then it twigs. He knew there was something about the containers up on that roof in the playground. They are here. They are in this garden. He's staring right at a pile of them. The same, but different. The ones on the roof were pots from this exact batch. Taken there by whoever tended this place.

This is Barry's garden.

Of all the painful realizations he has had, this one is the most upsetting. It leaves him mutely gasping for air. He knows none of it matters now, that his doesn't change anything, or make sense of anything, or undo anything. And he knows it's ludicrous that he even feels like this. But the unassailable fact remains – a part of him, however small or insignificant, has died. It has died and it won't ever come back to life. The plants around him that filled him with hope, with joy, with dreams of a future – that fed him, both in body and soul – those self-same plants are a living testament to his guilt. He takes them all in, one by one, the fruiting bushes, blooming flowers, thrusting saplings – he won't shy away from their accusations, nor will he deny them, leave them to wither and die. He will tend them. He must tend them. And just like that, he sees his future at last.

***

THE MAN

The days that follow blend into one. Not blissfully, but fitfully and fearfully. They are both exhausted by the new routine of waking and feeding, the burping and vomiting, the crying that puts them on edge - willing it to stop, praying it doesn't attract the attention of someone intent on doing them harm. The weather is mercifully warm. He leaves more pots out, and they are blessed by the occasional rains that replenish their supplies and double as an ad-hoc shower for the whole family. They sleep when they can, and when they are awake they are in a permanent daze. But the ring of thick, deep green that surrounds them keeps them safe – muffling the sound of their daughter's wailing, hiding them from prying eyes and even nourishing them with its smattering of edible berries.

He's picking berries from the hedge and daydreaming, or possibly just thinking (it's hard to differentiate these days), about how they imagined these first few weeks might be. New parents. At home in the mansion block atop the hill, with their marvellous views and their totally non-baby-proofed penthouse (for that, read 'top floor' more than 'executive suite') apartment. A thorn pricks the tip of his index finger, drawing a thick, dark drop of blood to the surface. He turns at the sound of their daughter stirring, the metallic tang of the blood still in his mouth. He knows the truth of it now. Nothing can prepare you for this. Perhaps it's better this way. They might not have survived this if it had happened before. Something about this place makes it possible. Lucy appears from the far side of the clearing, over by the spot they designated as the 'toilet' area. She walks over to the coarsely woven Moses basket - one of the first things he fashioned, from flexible green wood and lined with moss and grass - to lift their daughter up to her breast for yet another feed.

He approaches quietly, hands held out, cupping a meagre offering of berries. Her words bring him up a step short.

"I think we need to leave."

He can still taste a hint of iron, and looking down he sees the blood has trickled from his finger down onto the first of the berries.

"We can stay a bit longer."

"I don't mean we. I mean us. Me and her."

He doesn't understand. He just stands there, holding the blood-covered berries, mute.

"I'm sorry. But I need to take her away. From here. From you."

He still can't bring himself to speak.

"I didn't mean it like that. But... that is what I mean. I want to raise her myself. Just me. And not here. And I really think you should stay. I think you need to stay."

He takes the outermost berry, the one most infused with blood, and puts it in his mouth. It's a strange, but not entirely unpleasant sensation.

"I'll miss you. Both of you."

That may be the first time I've said that and it's been completely true.

***

11th December 2020

When I think about it, it's amazing how quickly you get used to it all really. It seems like a completely separate life when I was addicted to my smartphone, constantly checking it for any tiny update or notification, reliant on it for every scrap of information - how to walk somewhere I'd been to a million times before, what the weather was like beyond my curtains, how to boil an egg.

There's a release to being without all that information. It was paralysing to know it existed, was at your fingertips, all day and all night. Now I have to trust myself, my memory, my own logic and understanding. I can feel synapses growing and linking - the network expanding and rejuvenating.

It feels like... evolution?

***

LUCY

Their time in this curious little garden has been the strangest period she can remember, and that's saying something. She can't quite piece together all the events that brought the three of them here – just fragments of the horror of the walk from her house, the short and ill-fated ride in the ambulance, the crash, the hospital, the long trek here. Nor does she really even know where to start that story, for it certainly begins much earlier. But she does now know how she wants it to end, and it's not with the three of them living out their lives here. Nor is it with them leaving. At least not all of them. *She* needs to leave. And she'll never be separated from her baby. Never. But she can see already that *this*, whatever *this* is, will not work, is not sustainable. He may not be as quietly off-the-scale psycho as that poor man pretending to be a doctor, or as scarily, violently, temperamental as Barry, but just because he proved the best of a seriously bad bunch doesn't mean he's somehow back on track to be her life partner. He's damaged too. He was before, and he's even more so now. She can see it in everything he does. Everything except tending the plants. Only then does she catch a glimpse of the man she had once loved, a lifetime ago, when the world was different. A man who, back then, hadn't spent a waking moment gardening.

Funny.

She can see it is a shock to him, her words striking him dumb. He just stands there and eats those fucking berries. She knows she should be grateful but she's so sick of rainwater and foraged food from this claustrophobic green prison that she could scream, could claw at his eyes and stuff those berries down his throat. And that's why she needs to leave. And why he needs to stay.

And then miraculously he seems to get it. She sees him nod, his lips forming the words: *I'll miss you.* She could kiss him, cannot remember the last time she felt such a rush of gratitude and happiness, something even bordering on love. She recalls that this is how it used to be. Whenever they felt they'd got to the point of no return, or at least whenever *she* felt that, he'd found a way to be so uniquely him – the very best of him – that he'd brought it back from the brink. But those precipitous moments had happened more and more often, especially after the miscarriage, until it felt like their entire life was just careening from one flash point to the next. Trapped in that flat, unable to escape, the world burning and their lives unravelling. She'd had to leave then. But that had been different. The right decision, perhaps. But for the wrong reasons. And with the worst possible consequence – Barry. She reassures herself that this is nothing like that. And to her surprise she believes it.

Released from her guilt, and from her fear of this conversation, she's able to see him differently. She can appreciate the water, the food, the thousand tiny kindnesses and considerations he's paid her these last few days, can accept them for what they were – gestures of love, freely given. She can see that, beyond the strangely lean physique and curious hair and beard, he has softened somewhat over the days. But she can also sense something else, a new hard, dark core within him, a kernel of something irrevocable, irreconcilable. She knows when she first became aware of it, when he returned with the bucket of water however many days ago. And she knows now she may never learn what it was that caused it. But that black centre, that creeping darkness within him – *that* she knows is here to stay. And that is why she must leave. And, self-aware as ever, that's why he knows he must acquiesce.

He moves away, ostensibly to tend another part of the garden. And once more she is grateful. He's nothing if not sensitive to her needs, even now. She needs a moment to gather herself, sorting her feelings and putting them carefully back in their proper places, tidying away her emotional laundry. Their daughter – *how she needs a name!* – is thankfully suckling away, blissfully unaware of anything and everything.

Thank heaven she's a good feeder.

She realises she was so ready for a confrontation, so prepared to have to argue her case, beg, shout, demand, that she doesn't know what to do with herself now that he's just accepted it. She wasn't exactly spoiling for a fight, but it might have been a good way to release some hormonally driven tension and frustration.

She doesn't notice she has been pacing and fretting until the baby's cry alerts her to the fact that she's pulled her nipple away accidentally. As the feed resumes, she tries to calm down, walking evenly, breathing deeply, focussing her mind on the path ahead – her and Eve. Yes. *Eve.*

He's hovering again, she can sense him over her shoulder. It seems that will never go away, her ability to know he's there, to feel the vibrations he gives off. Becalmed, she turns to face him, and he takes an uncertain step forward as he speaks.

"I was hoping..."

"Yes?"

"That you'd let me name her."

And that's his superpower, the ability to get in there and say exactly whatever it is she's thinking about before she can do so herself.

Damn him.

"If that's OK?"

She tells herself she can always just ignore his choice once they leave, can choose to call her whatever *she* wants and he'll be none the wiser, even though deep down she knows she probably won't.

Probably.

"Errm... OK?"

"Oh great. Thank you. I just... I was... I was thinking about... maybe... Eve?"

Oh for fuck's sake. Here come the tears.

She feels her shoulders heaving as he moves to her side, can just about make out his words through her sobs.

"Oh god, I'm sorry! I'm so sorry! Please, Lucy, let's just... we don't have to... here, sit down."

And just like that she's sat on the floor at his feet, crying, rocking gently back and forth with Eve, their Eve, cradled in her arms.

As she gasps and fights to master her emotions he chunters on, digging the same hole, uncomprehending.

"We can change it. I just thought... well, I don't know what I thought. It just, it just seemed to fit."

Finally, she regains sufficient composure to reply.

"No. It's perfect. Eve. She's our Eve."

She smiles, and looks up at him to see it's his turn to cry, his face collapsing into a big, ugly, happy mess.

What a pair we are.

***

THE MAN

His nervous energy and finely tuned internal alarm clock wake him early, from a strangely untroubled sleep. Last night was the first when he did not dream of Barry, his head staved in by the seesaw; or Sanjay, hosting a tea party or dinner dance amidst the hospital corpses as the flames encircle them; or Mr. Singh, unravelling his turban to release his long hair in a cascade of blood; or of Tim, sawing off his own leg and tossing it to the hungry rats. Last night he had slept the peaceful, dreamless sleep of a man with a conscience balmed by the right decision - letting Lucy and Eve go.

The right decision. The only decision. Let them leave me and my ghosts behind.

Today is the day. He's up early to prepare. He wants to give Lucy and Eve as much of the bounty of this oasis as he can possibly muster. He'll only hold back enough to ensure the plants survive and can grow and reproduce, enough that he can eke out his existence here. But he has one important task to take care of first.

The park seems less threatening in the early morning, the dew not quite burned off, the sun not quite so oppressively hot. His mind feels clear, for the first time in an age.

Amazing what a good night's sleep will do.

He's able to navigate his way from the garden and through the overgrown grass, keeping the lurking, brooding presence of the hospital buildings to his left, always just in the corner of his eye, where he can make sure they don't leap out at him. He thought he was prepared but, when he reaches the playground, he realises he wasn't. Not even close. Even though Barry's body is no longer there.

He'd forced himself to do that days ago, to move it and eventually to bury it in a shallow grave in the scrubland on the other side of the playground, on the slope of the railway siding facing the hospital. That hadn't helped with the dreams. But he'd hoped it would mean that the power of this place was somehow reduced. It wasn't. Isn't. He can see

Barry everywhere he looks, but especially there, where the concrete is still dark, beneath the end of the seesaw.

He hurries on, tucking his chin into his coat, flipping up the collar into a makeshift pair of blinkers, closing down his peripheral vision and focusing only on the route ahead.

Back to the road.

It's only when he knows that he's out of sight of the playground that he realises he's been holding his breath. He takes a long, deep draught of the cool, crisp air – one of the few real, tangible benefits of the total collapse of their modern society. His injuries are more or less recovered, and he feels invigorated once more as his long strides take him through the trees and bushes and up to the low railings that mark the border of the park. He can see the road from here, and realises he must only be a few metres away from the spot where he first saw the ambulance, with Singh poised to strike. Should he have let him? Would he feel any different now? They might be two distinct flavours of guilt, but he suspects they'd have the same end result.

The ambulance is still there, what's left of it anyway. It's been scavenged to within an inch of its life, a hulking skeleton bleaching on the savannah. He surveys the road from his hiding place, conscious of the risk he's taking, desperate not to get caught out in the open again. There's no sign of anyone. Nothing he can see triggers his mental alarm.

Let's just hope it's still there...

He trots across the open road in the low crouch he affects whenever he's scared of being seen, keeping his centre of gravity low, ducking his head as far below the horizon as he can, like a cowboy avoiding being silhouetted on the high ridge line. He makes it to the ambulance without incident, and takes a second to squat on his haunches, his back against the side of the vehicle, to regain his breath and take another survey of the area from this new perspective. Still nothing.

He drops to his hands and knees, his muscle memory holding him centimetres above the ground in a press-up position, and turns his head to look under the vehicle. He feels the panic start to rise... and then - yes, there it is - the tell-tale rectangular outline of his diary. He crabs his way beneath the ambulance until he has the book in his hands once more, then lowers himself fully to the road, closes his eyes and just breathes in the pages.

A sound. Hard to tell how far. And again. Closer. Not yet right on top of him, but unlikely to be so far away that he can get out from under here and scamper back across to the park before whatever it is catches sight of him.

And then he sees them. A pair of boots. Black biker boots. Scuffing slowly along the road, coming straight towards him. He tucks the diary into the deepest pocket of his coat, presses his palms to the ground ready to move, and holds his breath.

The boots get ever closer. The steady scraping echoing, like nails on a chalkboard in a long-abandoned classroom. They stop right beside the ambulance, not two feet from where he lies. He tenses. A big, dirty hand places a pale blue glass jar on the ground. There are some mumbled words that he can't make out, the gruff timbre of the voice, even as it cracks with emotion, familiar. Then the boots turn around on the spot and begin their slow march away, back whence they came.

When he's finally sure he's alone again he crabs his way back out from under the ambulance. The makeshift vase contains a single sunflower.

***

28th March 2021

I'm probably mad to be writing another diary. The last time, when you read it, it really was the final nail in the coffin of our moribund marriage. Your act of reading it, and the things I had written in it - there was no coming back from that twin betrayal. I think I needed somewhere to work through my suspicions about you and Barry, knew I could never challenge you about it directly. And my cowardice extended to my inability to act on my attraction to the woman who reminded me of a younger version of you, who taught me how to make a fire and navigate using moss and mud. Something else I needed to write about. Perhaps, perversely, needed you to read about.

If it's you reading this again, Lucy, then I think we both understand by now. There's some solace in that.

If it's someone else turning these pages, a stranger, then I hope you won't judge me, or us, too harshly. Or maybe you should. Perhaps some judgement is what I need. It's certainly lacking in my existence now. Mr Tibbles is the closest I have to a conscience. Cats aren't the best moral compass in my experience.

***

LUCY

She's pottering around the garden like a nervous, broody mother hen when he gets back. Eve has only been asleep for a few minutes, and she's about to admonish him for a slightly less than totally silent arrival when she sees the expression on his face. It's almost enough to make her question her decision to leave. But not quite.

Instead, she moves towards him - and he interprets her intentions perfectly, meeting her halfway and collapsing into the hug. There haven't been many moments like this for a very long time, and she lets herself go with it. The embrace is just the right kind of tender – gentle but firm enough to show real support and emotion, and for once without any sense of misunderstood intentions. This is basic human love in its purest, most platonic form. A broken man in need of help, another human there to offer it.

They stand that way for what seems like an eternity. It can't be very long though, as Eve is still asleep when he gently extricates himself, and thanks her with a smile and the softening of his face.

"Would you be OK to stay one more night?"

She nods.

"Thank you. There's just... one more thing I need to do."

"Sure. We can leave tomorrow. First thing."

"Of course."

She hears Eve waking, and as she moves over to the makeshift basket he wanders away.

***

THE MAN

He spends most of the rest of the day tending the garden, gathering together as much of its bounty as he can afford to spare (perhaps even a little bit more) into a homegrown gift basket that wouldn't have been out of place in the world they used to inhabit, would have cost a pretty penny from the organic grocers on the thriving gentrified high street. Lucy sleeps when she can, normally just lying down beside the basket and drifting off atop the springy, green grass as Eve gurgles and whimper through incomprehensible dreams.

He takes the occasional turn holding his daughter over his shoulder - burping her or comforting her – as he passes through that part of the garden, or when Lucy needs to go to the loo. He knows it should feel special, should feel like bonding, but somehow it doesn't quite. He's not sure if it's because he wasn't there for the pregnancy or the birth, or because he knows he won't be there for her from now on, but all he really feels is a sense of melancholic detachment. Occasionally, as he holds her up, he gets that awful fear of dropping her (*throwing her?*) – that same spontaneous leap of imagination that leads us to wonder 'what if I just jump?' or 'I could step out in front of that bus'. He fights it down, piling the guilt he feels at the very notion on top of it, until it is buried beneath his own fear and self-loathing.

They're better off without me.

As Lucy returns, he fights the urge to immediately hand Eve back to her, instead turning away and bouncing her gently, whispering fragments of a half-remembered lullaby in her ear. When he thinks it's safe to pass her over without appearing negligent, he does so with a smile that he hopes seems warm and genuine, but fears looks weak and insincere.

It'll be easier when they're gone.

As the day fades away in a riot of yellow, orange, red, pink, purple and finally black he senses the wind whip up. Not so much in their hidden garden, within which the bluff of greenery maintains a duck pond calm, but in the erratic swaying of the upmost stray leaves and branches atop the circlet of trees - and by studying the stars and the way they are vanishing from the firmament in great swathes, as invisible dark clouds race across the sky. He senses a drop in temperature and then, on the very periphery of his hearing, the rising roar of the incoming rain as its earthward trajectory is interrupted by leaf and branch.

He rouses Lucy, and escorts them into the greenhouse as the heavens open. With no lightning, and the moon now obscured by cloud, their world shrinks yet further to become the few feet beyond their arms in the pitch black of the glass structure as they try to find a spot to lie down. The rain on the panes is almost deafening, like standing at the foot of a waterfall or beside an oil drum filled with firecrackers. Despite - or perhaps because of - the noise Eve, initially woken by their sudden retreat, is quickly becalmed, and soon asleep. Lucy reclines with Eve across her chest as he sits cross-legged beside them, listening – as he never ceases to – for any danger, any intruder. He knows he can't keep this up. He doesn't want to, but he can't help but feel gratitude and relief for their impending departure. Come tomorrow it will once more only be his own safety that he has to worry about.

A new noise arrives - insistent, metallic - causing Eve to snort and roll over. In the near darkness he hunts the source, desperate for their daughter not to wake and spurred on by the enervating nature of the sound that he knows will drive him mad if he can't stop it. As he stumbles through the greenhouse, trying not to bang a shin or stub a toe, or send something crashing down that will certainly end their child's slumber, he's reminded of when he was last here. Alone. A very different life. Something about being alone for all that time – okay, not such a long period in terms of months or years but, given the intensity of the situation, and the true nature of his isolation, a powerful removal from the world – something about it changed him. More than he could have envisaged, and in ways he can't put into words. But he can tell he will never be the same. Those months have rewired him. She knows it. He knows it. That is their new truth.

And there it is – a leak in the roof and the steady plink, plink, plink of water falling twelve feet onto the side of an empty tin can discarded on the floor. He picks up the can, squeezes its sides to work out the dent in it, tilts it at a fourty-five-degree angle and catches the next few drops of rain. When enough water sits in the bottom, he places it back on the floor where the metallic plinks are replaced by a drip-splash as it fills up. It's a sound that should be just as irritating, but that he long ago not only got used to but in fact celebrated. Water collecting has become his lullaby of choice, the closest thing to music in a world of silence.

The rainfall has eased and steadied, the patter less percussive and more like the gentle background roar of waves breaking on a shore. His eyes have adjusted to the dark, and he finds his way back to Lucy and Eve without incident, stopping a few feet away, as soon as he can make them out clearly enough to see their chests rising and falling. He is conscious of taking this moment to make the effort to commit this to memory; to study the light - how there is just enough of it to pick out the gentle curves of their bodies. To catalogue the sound of the rain, the smell of the place – the abundance of ripening, flowering plants, the scent of the damp grass beyond, the musty, steamy greenhouse incubating death and decay... and new growth, new life.

He just stands there. They sleep. The rain falls. The plants grow.

Finally, he tears himself away. He has a job to do, the last and most important, and it's likely to take him all night. First, he needs some light...

***

16th April 2021

What is the point of this diary? I have asked myself this question more and more often recently, as I sit down to write. Is it a letter to Lucy? Am I begging for forgiveness? For understanding? Is it a monument, my legacy, my vain attempt to leave something of myself behind in this ruined world? Am I confessing? Or explaining? Or teaching? Is it intended for some traveller far in the future, who might find it, uncover it like an artefact of an ancient religion, that it might help them understand what it was like for me, for all of us, who lived through the moments in which our civilization collapsed?

At first it seemed to give me hope, purpose. It seemed useful, somehow. Important. Now I'm not so sure. It feels like pure ego. In holding a mirror up to myself I'm revealing something not even I want to look at. Why on earth would anyone else?

Today is smashed every mirror in this flat.

I think I should abandon this diary.

***

LUCY

She's stiff and sore, awoken by a plaintive cry from Eve that could mean any number of things but she's pretty sure this time means 'feed me'. It can't have been long that they've been asleep, Eve wouldn't have allowed that, but there's enough of a glow from without to suggest the dawn is approaching. She realises how completely she's lost track of time, of minutes and hours – but also of days, weeks, months. Something about this new world can't help but leave her rudderless, cast adrift in a reality lacking all the aspects of a successful adult's existence.

None of that stuff matters any more.

Maybe that's why she'd left him. Maybe that's why she no longer wants him, or Barry, or anyone else for that matter.

Because it's not important.

Eve is all she needs. And, as long as she is enough for her, then this is the right thing. They can make their own future. She can see what that might mean for him – but she knows, in her bones she knows, that the darkness he is holding in will bleed out, will seep into her, into Eve, will poison them all eventually if they don't leave.

He's back from wherever he had pottered off to, looking exhausted, staggering slightly, as if he hasn't slept at all. Together they go about the ritualised preparations for departure, for separation, the essence of which haven't changed. It's awkward, stilted, both the same as, and nothing like, the last time. And yet...

This feels right.

She feels at peace, the certainty within her is reassuring, makes every step on this path one that strengthens her resolve and rekindles a hope she only now realises she had lost somewhere along the way.

He has fruit and vegetables, a collection of receptacles filled with fresh rainwater and a small knapsack that he presses into her arms when she puts Eve down for a split second to rest her aching back.

"Take it."

"Thanks. I think. What's in it?"

"Some duplicate tools, for gardening and other stuff. Some other bits and bobs I thought you might find useful."

"It's kind of heavy."

"I know. Sorry. But please, just take it."

"Sure. Listen, thank you. I... I..."

"It's OK. I know."

"She looks more like you I think."

"Really?" His face beams. "You think so?"

"Definitely. Your nose. Unfortunately."

He takes the jibe in the spirit it's intended.

"I'm sure I read somewhere that they often look more like the dad in the beginning. To keep us interested. Keep us around."

"Well, no luck there I'm afraid. Right, Eve? You're going to be a mummy's girl."

"She'll always be my little girl."

"Yes. Yes she will."

***

THE MAN

He guides them through the protective ring of green that encircles the secret garden for one last time, leading them back through the gate and below the arch that marks the entrance to his oasis. Back in the wilds of the park he sets a course that will take them to the border with the main road, but will maintain a safe distance from the playground and the hospital at all times. For now, he carries the knapsack, Lucy feeding Eve as they walk - if not leisurely then certainly not briskly, despite the purposeful nature of the journey.

The sun is still low, the long grass strung with iridescent necklaces of glinting dew, the heat of the day not yet upon them. Eve detaches herself from her mother's breast and hiccups, and they stop walking to marvel at the tiny thing they have created. There's joyful glint in her eyes as she speaks:

"Let's swap."

"Eh?"

"You carry her. Here, give me that."

Lucy holds Eve out to him and nods her head at the knapsack. He unslings it from his back, puts it down at her feet and grasps his daughter. As he burps their little girl over his shoulder, Lucy swings the bag over hers. They walk on like this for some time. He just gently patting Eve's back, unaware that she has drifted off to sleep, she taking a moment to clear her mind, to put her daughter's needs to one side, to forget him too, to just be in this wild park as the sun rises and the overnight rain and dew evaporate into the air or trickle into the earth, the water cycle's perfect circle uninterrupted.

The distant treeline slowly rises before them, the treetops growing, stretching, reaching for the heavens, as they approach the edge of the park. They stop in an uncanny unspoken unison, on either side of the shadowline cast by the low sun over the treetops. He in the shade, keeping Eve out of the sun, she in the full sun, soaking up the warmth like a lizard on a rock. She steps into the cool and he hands Eve to her.

"Straight through."

"I can manage."

"I know."

He watches them leave – Lucy's outline shrinking into the distance until it eventually blurs, inseparable from the outline of trees and bushes marking the edge of the park - and it feels like his whole life, his existence on this planet, has all been building up to this moment.

This is it. This is the real end... the real beginning.

He imagines himself lifted up, dripping wet and gasping from the river, childlike in the arms of the priest. Naked before his new God, despite the sodden white gown that clings to him.

As sadness threatens to overpower the relief he feels at his impending solitude, he conjures two thoughts to mind – the memory (image, sound, smell) of Lucy and Eve sleeping in the greenhouse as the rain hammers down, and the metaphorical trail of breadcrumbs he has stashed in the knapsack. The diary. His diary.

***

A Day in Early May, 2021

Dear Eve,

If you are reading this, or hearing these words read to you, then my first wish has already come true. Please give your mum a kiss and tell her thank you. The book that your mother should have given to you at the same time as this letter is my diary. I wanted you to have it, and to read it if and when you feel able. I have no idea how old you are now, but if you need to you can always get mum to help you with it. It might be a bit scary or confusing in places – I started it long before I knew about you, before you were born. But that's life – scary and confusing, in places. And I wanted you to know that life was scary and confusing before you were born too – that it always has been and always will be, and that we can still live and love and be happy even so.

I am writing this letter as we are preparing for you and your mother to leave. You were born just a few days ago, in a hospital I can just about see over the treetops from the wild garden in which I sit. It is the hardest thing I have ever done, letting you both go. But also perhaps the first really true, the first really right, thing I may have ever done. So the sadness I feel is not despairing, but hope-filled. This is a new start for you both.

I risked my life to preserve my diary, but it was only when I realised that I would be saying goodbye that I knew I had to give it to you. So that you can understand where you came from. So that you can perhaps understand why we did what we did, and that we did it all for you in the end. That you can perhaps find a way to forgive us, forgive me. And, and here I know I am dreaming, that you might one day decide – having read this letter and this diary – to come and find me, to give your old dad one last hug.

Know that I have dreamt of you every night, thought of you every waking moment of every single day, since we parted. You are the best part of me – and that is why I had to let you leave. I know your mother will have done her best to explain everything to you, I trust her completely to tell the truth of what happened to us and to you. But the words you will read in my diary come straight from me, for better or worse. I am sorry if any of them are hurtful, scary or painful to read. I hope they won't cause you to disown me. I hope that despite everything you will still think of me as your father. I dream of one day hearing you call me that. Father. Daddy. Dad. Anything. Just hearing your voice.

Be brave. Be strong. Be tough. Be smart. You need to be all those things and more just to survive in this world. But be kind. Be gentle. Be caring. Love. The world needs all those things and more if it is to improve. If anyone can help you find that balance it is your mother. Listen to her.

If it's safe, and if you want to, you can find me here still. I will never leave this place. I will always be here, waiting, hoping. Ready to welcome you. You have given me the gift of purpose. It is no exaggeration to say that you have saved my life. Even if we never see each other again, I will always know that truth. And now you do too. Thank you.

I love you.

Dad

***

THE MAP

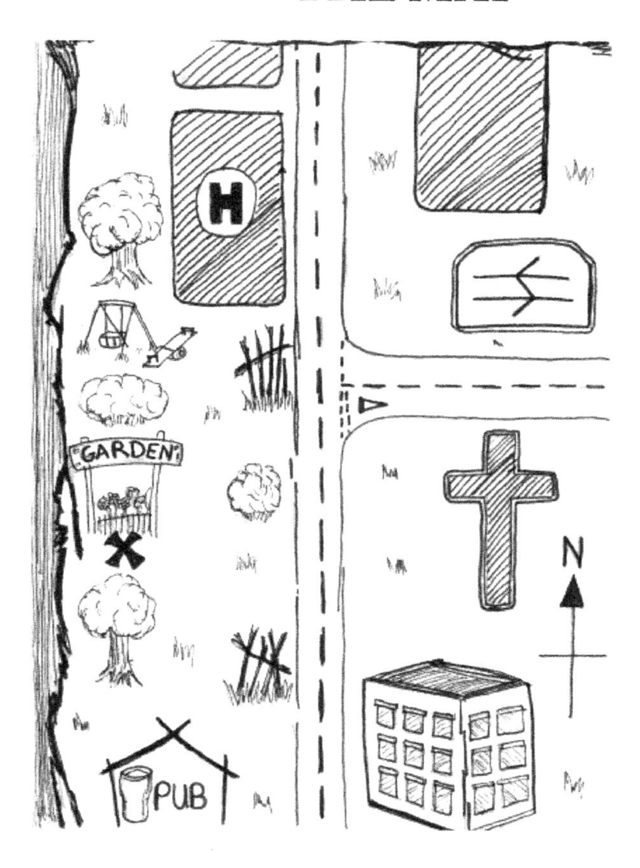

EVE

She has read it more times than she can count, ever since she was old enough to make out the words for herself, her mother grateful to finally hand over the grimy, torn, worn out pieces of paper and the unremarkable book that was the life and times, the confession, of her father – a man she has never met. At first it had been read to her as a kind of bedtime story then, as she got older, she was able to read along in parts, and finally it was hers and hers alone, her birth right. The letter – not the words of her father, but the condition of the paper itself – telling the tale of her own life. The smudges and stains of dirt, blood, food; the singed corners, the jagged rips and tears, the minor repairs; all with a story behind them - like the myriad different scars on her body that revealed her painful growth like the hypnotically concentric rings within the trunk of a fallen tree. She kept it with her always, never trusting it to what might pass for a safe place or hidey-hole in whichever spot they were living at that given moment. Even when they'd stayed somewhere for a bit longer, their transient life punctuated by occasional chance encounters and interactions that brought them, for a time, into a new community and even sometimes into a home, four solid walls, a roof... even then she had never squirreled the letter and map under a loose floorboard or in the back of an old wardrobe – although that had more often been the fate of the bulkier diary. No, the letter and the map were always on her person, tucked safely close to her skin.

She runs her fingers over the loose pieces of paper, their edges - rough and smooth - worn down by reading and folding and unfolding, ragged from fits of rage and desperate rescues. She consults the map a final time, then carefully folds the papers and slides them inside her coat once more. As she passes the old disused train station, she feels ghosts rise up around her, the knapsack on her back and the battered old diary within suddenly heavier, the worn out straps digging painfully into her slim shoulders. She moves light and fast, just like her mum taught her, in and out of sun and shade, flitting between the cover of wrecked vehicles and the generic scattered detritus of a collapsed world, the only world she has ever known. She's careful to keep the dark, looming skeletal hulk of the burnt-out hospital out of sight as best she can, harbouring a subconscious pseudo-spiritual belief in its power, in the ability of the negative energy it contains to curse her voyage. It stands like a giant cyclops - a creature one of the strange old men in one of the camps they had washed up in a few years ago had told her about, reading by firelight from a paperback book that looked even older and more decrepit than her dad's diary. She is desperate to stay out of the sweep of its all-seeing eye.

Her mother had travelled with her most of the way, unwilling to let her go the whole way across the city alone. It had taken a couple of days, slow going walking safely through the various zones that each presented a new challenge, a new threat, new risks. Too much for an eight-year-old, girl, no matter how tough and resourceful, no matter how determined, to manage on her own. Or so mum had said. She wasn't so sure. She was faster on her own. Mum was so cautious it slowed them down to a crawl in places. Plus, she was smaller and able to squeeze through tiny gaps and choke points. And mum had to stop all the time, coughing and wheezing, needing to 'have a little sit down'. But she'd been grateful when they'd had to take shelter and rest – they could take turns on sentry duty, and she only ever slept when she knew her mother was watching over her.

She is glad to be alone now though. As scared as she is walking here, where the horrific and barely conceivable events of the final scrawled pages of the diary play out a macabre dance like summoned spirits at the edge of her vision, she needs to do this herself. And she knows her mother, as much as she wanted to protect her all the way, could go no further. Not just physically, although it hadn't been a hard decision for them to make that she would remain at the last shelter point after a bad night during which her coughing had worsened (if such a thing were even possible), no - mentally, emotionally, it had been the only decision. She had always known that her mother would not complete this journey with her, that she could not go back to there, to him. She may only be eight, but she knows it is too difficult, too painful. She knows her mum still believes she made the right decision, has never stopped using it as a whetstone on which to sharpen her resolve, but that the self-same blade is one she uses to castigate herself, to cut herself, that this decision drives her mother just like her own self harm keeps her awake, aware, alive in this impossibly dark world.

She realizes she has reached the edge of the park, the bushes growing through and almost completely hiding the low railings, the trees gently swaying way up high above her head where a pair of crows harry a magpie, sending their pied relative wheeling away in defeat.

This is it. This is the park. Dad's park.

She walks slowly up the hill, searching for a thinning of the foliage, somewhere where she can push her way into the park, her mind keeping a mental tally of the distance, updating and redrawing the map she has long since memorised. Ahead she spies a darker patch - shadow, not leaves – where a large metal grate, some kind of drainage cover perhaps, has halted the inexorable creep of the plants. She hops over the railings before realising her mistake, the grate collapsing along pre-determined fault lines beneath her, tumbling into the pit below, the ear-splitting clang alerting anyone within a kilometre that something's afoot. She has just enough time to shoot out a hand and feel dirt beneath her fingers before the last of the grate falls away under her. Her fingernails snapping and breaking she digs in hard, barely slowing her fall until her hand snags in a knot of roots that spills from the soil out and over the hole. She hears her wrist pop as it arrests her momentum and takes her weight. But the roots hold, her wrist holds, and her descent is abruptly terminated. She bangs back against the side of the concrete lined pit, and all she can think is that she's grateful the knapsack is still on her back and not lost in the darkness below. She takes a beat to regain her breath, her composure, and then slowly, carefully, she hauls herself up, refusing to cry out despite the hot, sharp pain in her wrist, refusing to rush despite the fear of discovery. Her mother would be proud. Well, of how she got herself out, not how she got in in the first place...

***

EVE

It's getting darker. She knows that must mean she's been out here for hours now, even though it doesn't quite feel like it. She had been so determined to get there without looking at the map again - in her head she'd pictured the moment so many times and never had she needed to consult the route through the park. But now she has to admit to herself that she's lost. She's been going round in circles for some time, she's sure she was just in this strange clearing – the leering faces of the knotted trunks encircling her, spinning around and around and making her dizzy.

The next thing she knows she's sitting down, the map in her hands, turning the paper until it's orientated to the best of her understanding, holding it slightly away from herself to catch the last of the fleeing light as it retreats across the glade. Whatever happens she's leaving this place before dark, something about the trees makes her intensely uneasy. She banishes thoughts of her mother from her mind.

I've looked at the map, no excuses now, time to find him.

This time she pushes through a thicker, darker section, eschewing what she had taken to be an old path and instead striking out in the direction that she hopes is a straight shot, as the crow flies, to...

... the playground...

... and there, behind it, the blackened exoskeleton of the hospital. Two places that have been the recurring settings of the nightmares that have plagued her short life. Perhaps her mother should have kept the letter, the diary, from her. Perhaps such horrific tales shouldn't have been her lullabies. But no. The idea that she could be back there, back at the latest of a long line of places they tacitly agreed to call 'home', however temporarily, ignorantly living a lie within a community of strangers. Not knowing. That, to her, is the sicker thought.

She fights down the fear - of these places, of what they represent – bludgeoning it into submission with the blossoming realization that she now, finally, knows where she is. She gets out the map, desperate not to get lost again, her dream arrival already shattered. The sun has gone but, out in the open once more, a three-quarter full moon offers enough light on this cloudless night to make out the roughly sketched lines that point the way back to the garden, back to him. She's freezing, suddenly conscious of the drop in temperature and the chill now that she's standing still, her skin damp with the sweat from her exertions.

She turns on the spot, the map in front of her like a compass, or a water divining rod, until...

Yes! Yes yes yes! There it is!

The trees and bushes are huge but something about them, their shape, their growth, their lines, speaks of a human touch, a tender artistry working with, but not succumbing to, Nature herself. And the sign. The sign that has been a beacon in her dreams. Where the rest of the park is overgrown - the gates and railings, the fences and buildings, even the playground, strangled and suffocated by plants, trees, weeds - the sign is pristine. No letter obscured, no branch, leaf or vine allowed to cowl its message. It beckons to her, like the distant light calling a fisherman home.

***

EVE

It's the noise that she notices first. After the silence of the park, the cacophony of squawking and chirping seems deafening and completely surprising. But it stops abruptly as she steps out into the open of the garden – like a cricket that has sensed the presence of a potential predator. She sees a tree on the far side of the garden rippling in the wind.

No, wait, that can't be right.

The rest of the garden is as calm and still as a duck pond, protected from the elements by the thick belt of greenery that she had to push through to enter. Then the tree comes alive, the green leaves unfurling their wings and flying into the night sky, a flock of parakeets the size of which she has never seen before. The percussion of their multitudinous wings fills the air, then echoes away into nothingness as they disappear beyond the fattening moon.

She doesn't notice him appear. The garden, the birds – she is so distracted that she has failed to prepare herself. After all this, she isn't ready.

How stupid!

He must have been in the ramshackle sprawl of what was once a small greenhouse and is now a maze of offshoot lean-tos that give the whole structure the appearance of a flailing crystalline octopus. A door is slowly creaking closed, but he is right there, standing in the open in front of her, his long silver hair glittering in the moonlight. She stares, too scared to speak, to break the spell, to banish the ghost. He seems peaceful, serene – and yet there is an excitement in his eyes he cannot hide.

He's real.

"Hello dad."

***

EVE

Afterwards she won't remember ninety percent of what they talk about, something she will eventually castigate herself for - even more than her mother will. All she will recall is the garden.

He guides her around it like a living museum, pointing out the fruits and vegetables that he grew - first for himself, and then eventually to make up small boxes of produce that he would leave scattered in random places across the area for strangers to find. The roses – his first ornamental plants, that he has tended ever since deciding his food supplies were more than self-sufficient. His pride and joy, the crimson Japanese maple tree that he tells her once stood proudly in the communal garden of the block of flats where she had been conceived, and that he returned for one night, carefully digging up the tree and its entire root ball under cover of darkness and transporting it back to the garden.

At one point the parakeets return in a meteor storm of green and he explains how he had trained them to feed from that one tree alone, conceding his sour cherry crop to feed their voracious appetites but warning them away from any further encroachments with a few shots from his homemade slingshot. It seems like a fanciful story, a fairy-tale. Perhaps it is.

She feels dizzy, pleasantly so, a feeling she might in later years recognise as akin to being drunk, or gently high. It is like a whirling dance through the maze of a masquerade ball, her brow christened by a garland of flowers, a simple daisy chain they had carefully tied together.

And then... it ended.

She had always had an innate ability, a divine talent, for spotting the changes in other people's moods. The light in his eyes dims, his actions lose a fraction of their grace, what was smooth and natural becomes awkward, forced. She had always known she wouldn't stay. Her mother needed her too much. And, much as she had dreamt of this moment, she could not conceive of a future that did not involve her departure. Nevertheless, it still knocks her sideways when she feels the moment arrive. Her departure is as abrupt as her arrival, but they both seemed grateful to avoid a drawn out, awkward goodbye.

She turns to tell him how her mother had read his letter to her from the moment she could listen, that she herself had read his diary from cover to cover more times than she could count, that she wasn't afraid, or angry, or sad... but, before she can utter a word, she sees the flame rekindle in his eyes.

"Goodbye Eve."

"Bye Dad."

***

CODA

LUCY

She's been searching for Eve for what seems like hours.

Where has that girl got to?

Ever since they'd got back from The Trip she'd found her daughter had become more and more elusive, disappearing off to explore, to read her father's diary, to pick fruits and berries or tend to the 'secret garden' that she had created in fields just beyond the fortified walls of the encampment that had slowly become their home, a real home, its loamy soil beckoning them to put down their roots. She had been so sure Eve would have been at her constantly to take her back, or allow her to go on her own, to see her dad again. But there had been barely a mention of it in the weeks they'd returned. And yet the girl seemed re-energised, revitalised, reborn almost. A new surety, a confidence, that belied her tender age. She was blossoming.

A commotion in the distance washes over her in waves of distorted sound. A small crowd has gathered to welcome a new arrival. Rachel, a fellow mother and a true friend despite her gossipy nature, trots over, wiping her hands on her pinnie as she comes.

"Would you believe it! Just what we've been praying for – a doctor!"

Lucy's mouth turns , and she croaks out a nondescript entreaty as she gestures with her hands at the wicker bag under Rachel's arm. Her friend doesn't hesitate, pulling out a water bottle and tossing it over. As Lucy drinks she forces herself to breath slowly, to avoid choking and to calm her racing pulse.

It's been 8 years. What are the chances? It can't be him. It can't be...

"Funny looking chap. Charming, but hard to look at directly, what with all the scars and so on. Burns, I reckon. Poor fella."

***

ORTUM 2029

I cant put the days or dates on my diary entries like my dad did. Noone here keeps track ether. I was born into a world without a clendar. Mum had to explain how it used to be, in the time before I existed. It sounds terrible. I think it's much better like this – waking up with the sunrise, going to sleep wen its dark. Planting in spring, harvesting in ortum. Eating only what you can grow. Everybody nowing ther job and ther role. Mum says she likes it too. She says she never lived in a proper community before.

She dusnt no about this diary. I no she felt she had to read dads words to me, then teach me to read them myself. And she nos all us kids are learning to rite from Sally. She calls it 'skool'. But I don't think she nos I'm riting like this, like dad did. I don't think shed like it. I dont think she wants me to be like him. Shes not happy about my little garden – even though I know shell be proud enuff when I can share my harvest with the others. Shed freak out if she new about the diary. My diary.

I can hear her now, calling my name. I should probably go, she sounds weird – her voice has gone all high and scratchy, breaking up like the old radio transmitter they still insist on using here every day just in case someone radios back. She sounds like she did when we went to see dad.

I didnt want to when I first came back, but I think I might like to go back and see him again. Not for a while yet, but ventually. I should probly start planning that soon.

I'll rite more later if I can, but its getting harder to sneak away and to hide it from her, and its getting darker earlier too. She's really screaming now. Time to go. Bye!

THE END...?

BONUS MATERIAL

Will Corona return?

Perhaps with more adventures for our emerging young heroine, Eve?

That's up to you...

I've got a tonne of other stories bubbling away BUT if you want more of Corona, then let me know – I've got an idea for a sequel, so with enough appetite I might just make that my next big project...

So, if you enjoyed this book please do leave a rating or review on your platform of choice. Your feedback and support makes a world of difference and might just inspire others to read my work – so spread the word!

And I'm very active on social media – so please feel free to pop by my Twitter, Instagram, or my Facebook author page and say hi!

You can find links to all my socials, and much more, here:

https://linktr.ee/DavidArrowsmithAuthor

CORONA : THE SPOTIFY PLAYLIST

That's right, I've even created a music playlist on streaming platform Spotify – it's packed with songs that fit the mood, setting and plot of the book. So why not check it out and immerse yourself in the music?

LINK: https://open.spotify.com/playlist/2uuiGZj0scoca9ZYKesova?si=lFQCY_JnRgKiFLo2ELnxXQ

Other books by David Arrowsmith:

Nevada Noir : A Trilogy of Short Stories

- Top 10 Crime Reads of 2020 - Murder, Mayhem & More
- Top 10 Books of 2020 - Bedside Book Review
- Recommended by Number 10 Bookshop - one of the UK's only specialist crime fiction book stores

"brutal and beautiful, like a Dodge Charger kicking up dirt and grit as it tailspins away and disappears in a cloud of grimy dust"

"turbo-charged crime-em-up that kicks like a shotgun to the heart"

"a powerful novella of greed, brutality, despair... a superb debut"

"Stunning."

In the world of Nevada Noir, no one gets out clean...

In these three dark and brooding short stories, set in and around the US state of Nevada, a cast of disparate characters struggle with greed and temptation, and the cursed lure of easy money...

...an old man goes in search of his son in the aftermath of a terrible storm, a couple down on their luck make a life-changing discovery and an ex-cop has one last impossible decision to make...

Are you brave enough to take a trip to the badlands today?

Set in the barren scrublands of Nevada; the neon glow of Sin City Las Vegas; and the stark, deadly beauty of Zion National Park in Utah; Nevada Noir is perfect for fans of authors like Elmore Leonard, James Ellroy, Cormac McCarthy, James Sallis, Raymond Chandler, Chester Himes, Lee Child, Martin Cruz Smith and Roberto Bolaño - and of genres including noir, neo-noir, western, neo-western, pulp fiction, southern gothic and crime and detective fiction and mystery.

Grab your copy today, and immerse yourself in the brutal beauty of these three twisted tales.

http://mybook.to/NevadaNoirTrilogy

Coming soon:

The Drowned by David Arrowsmith and Christina Gustavson
(read on for an *exclusive* extract from this new novel)

In the works:
Nevada Noir Zero by David Arrowsmith

And lots more – follow me on social media for the latest updates.
https://linktr.ee/DavidArrowsmithAuthor

Acknowledgements:

This book begam life as entries in the Notes app on my iPhone during the initial lockdown of the Covid-19 pandemic in 2020. They were my attempt to catalogue, process and record the extraordinary events that were unfolding. Eventually I hit upon the idea of turning this factual diary into a fictional account – inspired by my love of the dystopian, in fact 'Ballardian', fiction of J.G. Ballard.

At the time, I was living in a small garden flat in East Dulwich, South London, with my wife Irma and our daughter Ivy – to whom this book is dedicated. They are my everything.

I credit my love of literature, of film, of stories, to my parents John and Carolina, they put me on the path I am on today and I owe them everything.

I also owe a huge debt of gratitude to all my friends and family, to industry friends especially Kirsty Milner whose support of my writing gave me the confidence to pursue my dream – and especially to many of the wonderful members of the writing community on Twitter. The support I have received from so many people following the release of Nevada Noir gave me the courage to push on and continue with my writing – and to publish this very book. So thank you, one and all – you know who you are.

One of those champions is fellow author David Wilby. Not only does he write excellent science fiction, but he's also a talented artist – as evidenced by the wonderful map included in this book, which is the work of his fair hand. Thanks David, you're a gentleman, a scholar *and* an artist. I designed the cover art myself - choosing, combining and editing images by talented photographers on the free stock sties pix-abay, pexels and unsplash.

I'm grateful to so many people. I hope my continued writing brings you a fraction of the entertainment and pleasure you all have given me.

David

An exclusive extract from this soon-to-be-published Scandi-Noir detective-versus-serial-killer thriller...

THE DROWNED
BOOK ONE
of
THE KJÄLLSTRÖM CYCLE

David Arrowsmith & Christina Gustavson

CHAPTER 1

His first thought is that she must be dead. No way that she'd be lying out in the snow this early in the morning by choice. The sun is barely up and it is still bitterly cold, a multitude of frozen crystals glistening in the light-kissed patches of bright white. She is half in and half out of the light, her body lying across a dark bar of shadow cast by one of the giant pines. The scene would have been magical, should have been the start to the day he needed, but the presence of the girl changed everything.

With a flick of the wrist he tosses his coffee out onto the pristine snow as he takes one last deep pull from the hand-rolled cigarette and crushes it out on the porch handrail. He feels a worrying twinge in his back as he stoops to pick up his winter boots from the corner where they have sat, unused, for rather too long. He pulls them on and steps down into the snow, silently cursing himself for not clearing the path for so long. He forces himself not to run, no need given she is almost certainly dead. His brisk long-legged stride propels him along deceptively fast, but as he steps off the hidden path he sinks knee-deep into the virgin powder. Well, he's certainly wide-awake now.

She is on her back, small and light enough not to have sunk too far down into the snow. Only a thin dusting covering her, a veil that merely blurs rather than disguises her appearance. The snow has partially melted around her, then refrozen in larger, smoother icy crystals. For a second he just stands and looks at her, her elfin beauty like something from Arthurian legend. That is his second thought - a fleeting fancy that she is Guinevere. Closely followed, and obliterated, by his third - that he is old enough to be her grandfather, and no King Arthur.

You've been reading too much.

Her chest moves. Only a fraction, it would have been imperceptible if it hadn't triggered a tiny avalanche of snow that cascades from the thin zipped up hoody that is her woefully inadequate protection from the elements.

The snow cleared from her face, her chest, with one tender sweep of his forearm, he breathes air smoothly into her lungs and pushes down on her rib cage. He keeps going, the training taking over, a trance-like state descending over him, somehow keeping him calm despite this shocking intrusion into the cocoon he had built for himself. He can feel the sun on his neck now, a pleasant warmth that brings a slow creeping smile to his face and a softening sparkle to his eyes.

Something about this place is indeed magical.

And then the cough. The ugly, beautiful cough of a body's internal engine spluttering back to life. Wild-eyed, vomiting up great mouthfuls of what seems to be dirty water, she starts to sit up, but he hugs her gently to his chest and lowers her back down to the snow with a whispered hush in her ear - as if he is putting a baby down to sleep. She's weak enough to allow it, and he shushes reassuringly as he feels around her skull and neck for the hot bumps of major swelling, the sharp points of bone marking a compound fracture or the rough, sticky patches of congealed blood from an open wound. Nothing. Just wet clothes, wet skin, wet hair.

She's cold, but not as icy as he had feared. Her fingers are blue and bring him out in goosebumps where they trail against his bare skin, but he can just about sense a gentle warmth still preserved deep in her core as he gathers her up in his arms and gently holds her limp form to his chest.

He wades back through the snow, doing his best to retrace his steps and plant his feet back in his own giant footprints. He's almost at the cabin when he stumbles on a tree root. He nearly falls, nearly drops her. She's jerked back awake, her eyes take him in, a look of faint confusion, and then they close again.

In the cabin he lays her down gently on the bed, strips the wet clothes off her and dries her carefully with the only towel he owns. He takes extra care around her wrists and ankles, where the skin is red and raw. He covers her in two thin blankets, then gingerly steps around to the other side of the bed and retrieves an armful of his own clothes from where they lie dumped on the floor, the walk-in wardrobe of the solitary male. He artlessly drapes the assorted items of clothing – a chunky cable knit cardigan with more than one sizeable hole, an old varsity style hoodie from his days at the academy, a faded pair of navy blue sweatpants – over her sleeping form, each one a further layer of insulation, no matter how desperately in need of a wash.

He carefully lifts and carries an ancient birchwood rocking chair over to the bedside and places it down silently, then adjusts the patchwork pillow in the small of his back and settles in. He watches the covering of clothes and blankets rising and falling gently, as he subconsciously rocks the chair in time with her breathing. His hands grip the armrests where the wood is smooth and shiny, the patina fractionally darker, his knuckles whiter.

CHAPTER 2

He's not sure how long he has sat there, rocking and watching, but it must be a couple of hours at least as he can feel the warmth of the midday sun on his cheeks – and the shakes returning to his aching hands. He's torn, for once feeling like he might have a reason to resist. Before he is forced to make the decision she grunts and rolls over, opening her eyes.

"Hey."

He's so eager to whisper softly that the word half catches in his throat.

She flinches, he can see her muscles tighten as she sees him and seemingly braces herself. When he doesn't move, makes no attempt to get up or approach her, but merely smiles gently, he sees her relax infinitesimally. He watches as her eyes take him in, then scan the room, their unsubtle movements alternating between skittish and lazy, out of keeping with the precise beauty of her face but unsurprising given her weakened constitution. She flexes her arms, and gently rubs at her wrists.

"It's OK. I found you out there, in the snow."

His voice, the breaking of the silence, turns her rigid once more. She stares at him intently, defiance, a hint of anger perhaps, in her eyes. He tries again.

"You don't need to worry. You're safe now. I'm a cop. Was a cop. Well, it's complicated."

She looks confused, but less scared. His bumbling efforts at calming her, his social skills already dwindled after only a few months of near isolation, seem to be having a positive effect.

"Don't worry, I don't need to know anything. Just rest and get better."

Her eyes once again take a tour of the cabin, a fraction more focus in their deliberation this time, the fear in her face slowly replaced by curiosity and then what he can only think is a spark of recognition.

"It's you. You're that cop who -"

"That's right."

His interruption is too swift, too certain, and he sees her retreat back into her shell once more.

I used to be better at this.

He tries a different tack.

"Next time maybe stick to the daytime for making snow angels."

She smiles at the weak joke - her frame, and her eyes softening the tension draining from her, from the room. He sits, doing his best to smile and project a sense of calm, of reassurance. Finally she yawns, a feline stretch toppling the cardigan onto the floor.

"Oops."

Her voice is hoarse but he can sense a clarity there, like a fine thread now frayed at the edges.

"You look better, anyway. Than you did."

"I don't feel it".

"Can I get you anything?"

He can see the hints of thoughts cycling through her head, the gentle twitching of her face revealing the existence, if not the substance, of her internal monologue. She shivers.

"A bath maybe?"

He's relieved she's requested something he might just about be able to muster up – and that she clearly hasn't spotted the condition of his old tub, or she'd never have asked. He's suddenly painfully aware of the state of his larder and of his home in general.

"Of course. Just give me a minute."

"I'm not going anywhere."

He retreats to the kitchen where he puts the antique cast iron kettle on the stovetop along with two big pans of water and sets them all to boil, then crosses the room to open the door and retrieve a bucket of icy cold water from the butt outside. This he tips into the dusty, dirt-streaked clawfoot bathtub that broods in the corner. Next he carries the kettle and pans over to the bath in two trips, pouring them in slowly and testing the temperature of the bath water as the competing currents eddy and merge.

When he's satisfied he heads to the door.

"I'll be just outside if you need anything."

The fresh air, brought slow and deep into his lungs, regenerates him. He feels like his cells are repairing themselves. This is why he came out here in the first place. Well, one reason.

He hears a gentle splash, and his heart stops for a millisecond. He opens the door and can't see her above the rim of the bath. Two strides take him to the tub. Her nose and mouth are just above the surface of the water, her legs just long enough that her feet touch the bottom edge – where they must have arrested her slide. Her chest is rising and falling, lifting out of the water before retreating beneath it once more, the water taking her weight, holding her suspended in its tepid embrace. The relief that washes over him in a wave is exhausting. He checks her hands – they're cold, and extremely pale, but no longer as icy or blue.

Her hair floats around her face like strands of seagrass. She seems at peace. Suddenly the scene is so familiar, so shocking and painful, that he feels himself about to vomit. Then she stirs, and that lazy smile comes to her lips, and he's able to fight the burning bile back down his throat.

It's not her. This isn't that.

He closes his eyes, forces the red and purple and green splotches that dance across the darkness to slow, and fade, until all he can sense is the blank black. He opens his eyes again. The girl is there, in the bath. A stranger. Alive.

He retreats back to the porch, his shaking hands making messy work of rolling a fresh cigarette from the tin on the rail. He stares out at the trees, not willing to turn back to check on her again. Eventually he hears a slosh and then the careful padding of damp feet back to the bed. He rolls another cigarette.

CHAPTER 3

The afternoon retreats and dusk creeps across the clearing. As the girl sleeps in Gustav's bed, wrapped carefully, but not too tightly, in the assortment of musty old blankets and stained clothing, he does something he's not done since he retreated out here – assess the cabin with the eyes of an outsider.

Better get to work.

He tidies books, papers, files and folders away; unpins maps and photos from corkboard wall panels; dumps rancid and mouldy food in the bin, dirty dishes in the sink and empty bottles in a wooden crate. One or two still hold some last remnants of their precious nectar, and he swigs at them as he goes, the bottles clinking pleasingly in his unsteady grip. Warm flat beer, wine turning to vinegar, and finally a good slug of rye whisky to cleanse the palate ...

... the three course meal of the alcoholic.

He smiles wryly at the thought. He knows it. He's self-aware enough to see he's become the cliché. And the truth of it is enough to perpetuate it. Knowing you're an alcoholic isn't the first step to salvation, it's just another reason to hate yourself.

I'll drink to that. Skål.

The bottle is empty, but at least his hands are almost steady, and the fire is still going strong as he pulls his coat tighter around himself and stares at the girl sleeping in his bed. She does look a bit like her, but not that much. Maybe he's been out here alone too long. He can feel the spectral memories tugging at his subconscious again now though. It's been a while, he'd almost forgotten their wraith-like power. They've been awakened, and he knows only one way to deaden their siren call. But the bottle is empty.

He tiptoes to the door, not wanting to wake her. Perhaps not wanting to be caught. Out of the door and around the back of the cabin and he's there, stood before the still. He fills the tankard carefully, holding his hand as steady as he can, fearful of spilling a single drop. As darkness falls, and the moon ascends, the thin stream of liquid glistens like quicksilver.

Hembränt.

Back inside she sleeps, and he drinks. The icy fingers of his past retreat slowly. The *hembrän*t is powerful stuff. This is his very first batch, and this the first taste. He's pleased with the effect so far. It seems to pack even more of a punch than the rye. The burn is rough and raw, but it at least it avoids the tell-tale taste of *finkel*. He can feel the warm glow spreading; the cold, clutching fear loosening its grip. He sees her stir, an errant strand of hair falling across her face. He gets up to move it away, but as he stoops over her she wakes – and he freezes, anxious not to terrify her. But the scream doesn't come, instead her face takes on a quizzical expression, her nose and brow wrinkling in tandem.

"What's that?"

"Eh?"

"That smell. What are you drinking?"

"Ah. It's... it's *hembränt*."

"You a moonshiner?"

"I guess so!"

He laughs. Perhaps the first laugh this cabin has heard in a decade.

"Gimme."

To hell with it, why not.

He passes her the smudged tumbler, the viscous and misleadingly clear liquid leaving alpine peaks and troughs up its sides. She raises the glass in a silent salute, and sips, the fiery booze catching in her throat and causing her to cough. Before he can rush to her aid she recovers and laughs.

"It's not my first drink, honest!"

There's that smile again. He feels a warmth, a peace, he's not felt for a long time. She sees off the rest of the glass, hands it back to him, rolls onto her side and closes her eyes. Back in the chair he just has time to count five of her inhales and exhales before he too drops off.

He's underwater, in a cool, clear lake. The water is peaceful as he slowly sinks to the bottom where the eelgrass waves and undulates around him, bathing him in its reflected emerald glow. He's cold. The sun must have gone behind a cloud way up above, as the water is suddenly darker, the grass a more menacing shade of green. It snaps and tugs at him. Long strands of jade wrap around his ankles, his wrists, his throat. He's choking, gasping for air.

He coughs out the hot, lumpy mess of his last meal from his oesophagus, the *viltgryta* as unappetizing on the way out as it had been on the way in. He used to love venison, but this had been an old and rangy deer and the meat had been on the turn by the time he'd made the final batch of stew. He gasps with relief, only to find the next wave upon him and another mouthful spattering onto the bare pine boards of the floor. Then he hears it. The cough, gurgle, choke from the bed. She too is choking, vomiting in her sleep. Not the deer, then ...

The hembränt.

His fingers prize her mouth open, scooping the nondescript chunks of white, pink and orange from her mouth and throat. As he tips her forward over his knee she wakes, vomits, coughs, spits and breathes. That's twice now. He's not sure he's got a third time left in him.

He stands and backs away slowly to give her room. She vomits again. She looks like death. He steps, barefooted, in a pile of his own sick. When he vomits again he's sure he can see fresh blood. She can barely sit upright as she wretches and pukes, bent over double on the edge of the bed and in danger of toppling over. He's burning up, desperate for cool, fresh air. Like clouds parting, his epiphany arrives. He takes two long strides, crouches down and picks her up. Tossing her over his shoulder he stumbles out of the cabin door and into the night.

Printed in Great Britain
by Amazon

24518499R00118